A Rare Connection: Inspirational Romantic Suspense

S.V. Farnsworth

Published by Stone Wolfe Press, 2020.

A RARE CONNECTION: INSPIRATIONAL ROMANTIC SUSPENSE

First edition. February 7, 2020.

Copyright © 2020 S.V. Farnsworth.

ISBN: 978-1733859974

Written by S.V. Farnsworth.

Also by S.V. Farnsworth

Modutan Empire
Woman of the Stone
Monarch in the Flames

Standalone
A Rare Connection: Inspirational Romantic Suspense

Watch for more at https://svfarnsworthauthor.com.

Table of Contents

A Rare Connection is dedicated to my husband, Reuben Farnsworth. He is the love of my eternal existence, the father of my children, and the man of my dreams.

Chapter One

"**A**ny news from the private investigator, Bertrand?" From the backseat, Nicole Moreau drummed her clearcoat nails on the armrest of the parked Rolls-Royce.

Smartphone in hand, the lanky family driver twisted to face her with a raised eyebrow. "Non, Mademoiselle. Now tell me again why you think chasing this boy half-way around the world is a good idea."

The censure caused her lower-lip to tremble. "It's the worst idea I've ever had. But it's my only chance, and I have to take it."

Bertrand's graying brows eased from harshness into a resolute expression. "Don't worry. No matter what he says, seeing you will make him happy. It always has."

"Thank you for saying that." The months apart had made her doubt.

With a sigh, she leaned back in the seat. The aroma of fine leather laced with the smog from ten lanes of traffic soothed her anxiety. She'd never been to Korea, even though her mother traveled here often.

Nicole had hired a P.I. to find Andrew Leavitt because...well, because she could. She missed him. Andrew's joyful nature had warmed her soul with radiant heat since they were twelve.

Unfortunately, she'd taken him for granted. Religion, which she had considered irrelevant, had whisked him away to South Korea. He'd already served as a missionary for eighteen months. But he had six more to go before he returned to his home in California. By then she would be in France attending graduate school at the Sorbonne in Paris.

Thus, she'd come bearing a small black box. Tomorrow was Christmas. It was the excuse she needed to muster the courage to offer Andrew everything.

"The investigator reports that Andrew has just arrived by bus." Bertrand pointed out the window.

A tall Caucasian man in a black fleece overcoat strode past. Andrew's long legs took him through the smartly dressed crowd. He entered a shopping center with a subway station underneath.

Without thinking first, Nicole flung open the car door and knocked over a middle-aged Asian man. She dove after him to break his fall. When their eyes met, she knew he was dangerously angry but hadn't been seriously hurt.

"Are you all right?" She spoke English thinking that would be the best since she didn't speak much Korean.

A canister had skittered away among the pedestrians and he lithely moved to retrieve it, going with the flow and disappearing without a word. Bertrand jumped out of the car and pursued the man. She gathered herself and followed Andrew even though there was no way of knowing where he went.

Careful this time, she hurried into the shopping center in pursuit of the man she loved. A missionary wasn't likely to be here to buy things but to catch a train. She hurried past the gaudy, gilded fountain and through a maze of shops to Jamshil subway station.

Since he was tall, she eventually discovered him. He was coming out of a pungent smelling restaurant. That made sense because it was lunchtime.

A throng of people stood between them.

"Andrew!" Nicole called.

He kept walking.

She followed him down a set of steps only to pull up short. The landing by the tracks was compacted with people. She tried to reverse course only to be mobbed and carried further into the tightening throng on the subway platform.

"Andrew!" Over the muffled voices and scuffling shoes, her voice sounded like a gunshot.

He looked in her direction, his body wedged in place. Scanning the crowd, his gaze finally rested on her. His chin tilted downward and his blond eyebrows shot up. He waded through the people, drawing close, though out of reach.

"What are you doing here, Miss Moreau?"

Nicole glared in annoyance at his formal use of her last name. But she enjoyed hearing his smooth baritone. She had missed the sound of his voice.

"I was in town and happened to see you walking by." She flashed a smile. "I thought I'd say hello."

She reached for the black box in the pocket of her gray slacks, but it wasn't there. She must have left it in the Rolls Royce. Her plans to propose marriage withered under the heat of her embarrassment.

His eyes narrowed in apparent suspicion. "You really shouldn't have come. It's against the rules."

Anger replaced embarrassment and her cheeks flushed with additional heat. She glanced from side to side at the tightening group of people around her, aggravated by an elbow in the ribs. Why was Andrew being such a jerk? She compressed her lips.

"Then, you don't want me here?" She desperately hoped that wasn't the case.

He ducked his head. "I didn't say that."

To her surprise, he blushed. Unbuttoning his heavy coat, he revealed a white shirt and a hideously plain and stained tie. She clenched her jaw at the sight of his threadbare clothes. He'd lost weight and his hairline had receded into a shallow widow's peak easily seen due to his unfashionably short haircut.

"You look awful. Don't they feed you around here?" Truth be told, she had worried for him.

It hadn't been her intention to offend him. In the eight years they'd known each other, she'd only seen him angry once. Now twice.

Additional color flushed his neck and face. He avoided meeting her gaze and his nostrils flared. His brows crashed together and his lower lip protruded.

"Don't throw a fit. It's the truth." Unable to strike the indignant pose she wanted; she jostled the people around her.

"What do you know about truth?" His eyes flashed. "You don't have a clue why I'm here, but you could have." He spoke in a whisper that barely carried over the heads of the people pressed between them. "You could have understood...if you wanted."

His expression softened. It filled with emotions she recognized such as sadness, regret, and loss. He looked away at an incoming train.

Brakes screeched as it came to a stop. The doors did not open. People pushed, forcing everyone toward the unopened doors of the nearest subway car.

"Ouch." Nicole's voice squeaked as she struggled against the surge of bodies.

Andrew sidled through the crowd to close the last bit of distance between them. His lips were pressed into a thin line and his blue eyes looked like steel.

"You shouldn't be here. Where's Bertrand?"

The mob crushed them together. She breathed in Andrew's familiar pine-fresh scent. The noise and press of bodies made her dizzy. She needed Andrew. Bertrand couldn't help with this.

"He's in the car," she answered.

"Did he follow you?" Andrew scanned the crowd.

"I don't know." Her voice came out weak.

She wanted to rest her head on his chest. But she refused to show vulnerability. Instead, she shut her eyes and tried to drown out the surrounding people.

"Bertrand, I have her," Andrew yelled. "Meet us at the embassy."

Her eyes flew open.

"All right." Bertrand waved good-bye.

He departed from the top of the nearest stairway. He hadn't been completely blocked in, though no one on the landing had any hope of escape.

An announcement blasted across the speakers in Korean. Nicole didn't understand more than a few words of it. However, the tension in the male voice conveyed a universal, spine straightening message of outrage.

The crowd hushed and the struggle abated as people listened. She imagined every other word as an expletive, though no one in the crowd reacted. Abruptly, the voice stopped and the train exited the station without opening the doors.

"What's wrong?" She asked.

Many people teetered precariously close to the edge of the landing. A woman nearly fell onto the tracks, but recovered and pushed against the masses. No one said anything.

"I'll find out." Facing away, Andrew spoke to an Asian man beside him.

She didn't know he spoke Korean this well. For the first time, she noticed both of them wore black name badges. She guessed they were friends.

That jogged a memory. Andrew's mother had mentioned that missionaries always worked in groups of two or three. They called it a companionship.

"It's a strike, I think." He frowned.

"Great." Her stress level escalated.

Another train rushed into the station, swirling the lady's hair. It stopped. The conductor made a calm announcement before the doors slid open.

People crammed her and the missionaries into a subway car. Along the line, the doors slammed on men and women who were only halfway inside. She winced at the sight of torsos, arms, and legs wedged between the rubber padded steel.

She and Andrew were lucky to have caught the train. At the same time, they were pitifully unfortunate to have been forced by the mob into the car because it was incredibly cramped. As soon as the doors cleared, the train departed from the station.

Chapter Two

Nicole couldn't breathe, despite being close to Andrew's calming presence. Patience, though strained, seemed to be the silent consensus of the other passengers in the subway car. She tried to match them and remain calm.

The heat and indignity of this many people pressed together felt like a hot, garlic sandwich. It made her dizzy. She was fortunate not to have a coat. Sweat beaded on the other passengers' faces. They wore heavy winter gear. Her heart rate increased and her breathing shallowed.

"I'm afraid I'm a bit claustrophobic." Her voice echoed in her ears as if underwater.

"I know." Andrew's gaze darted around the car.

Clearly, everyone was equally confined. To her relief, Andrew reached his arms around her and backed the people away ever so slightly. Now she could breathe more freely.

Overwhelmed, she leaned her head on his chest. Eyes closed, she tried to shut out the situation. Andrew's heartbeat steadied her nerves. But his arms trembled with the prolonged effort to give her more space than anyone else had. She knew it wasn't fair.

Regardless, she couldn't help feeling oppressed by the presence of this many people crushing in on her. She could barely maintain her self-control. Without Andrew, she would have panicked.

"You really shouldn't put your head on my chest. It isn't

appropriate." He spoke gently, though audibly enough for the people around to hear.

The car slowed to a stop, sending everyone crashing to the front. Only a few people struggled to escape. Then the train accelerated and people shifted rearward, this time crushing those at the back.

She released her hasty hold around Andrew's middle and lifted her head. No one spoke. But judging by the faces of everyone in the subway car, she and Andrew were being taken note of. She concluded that missionaries must have a lot of rules.

With each stop, a few more passengers debarked the train and a few less entered. Andrew dropped his arms, taking a half step away from her to grab a subway strap. Sweat dripped along the side of his face. He wiped it with a white handkerchief from his pocket and took off his overcoat. She noticed another black name badge clipped on his suitcoat pocket.

"Elder Leavitt?" She wondered what the Elder part meant because his name was Andrew Martin Leavitt, not Elder.

"It's a title. The girl missionaries are called Sisters." Distracted, he faced the other missionary.

"Girl missionaries?" She shot him a wry smile. "Do you think they're your sisters?" The whole missionary thing seemed absurd. Who did these people think they were?

"Yes." He frowned at her. "That's exactly how I think of them." He faced away.

"Then some cute missionary isn't the reason you've traveled halfway around the world?" Only after the words slipped out did she realize how accurately they described her foolish actions.

"Of course not." His head shook. "Now, excuse me, I have to find out how to take you to an embassy, either French or the United States. I don't even know if they have a French Embassy in Seoul." He spoke to the other missionary.

"You could ask me." Angered, her cheeks flushed with heat.

Why was he acting like this? What had happened to the boy she'd known or the teenager she thought had been in love with her? The man before her had changed. She respected his confident air. Except that now, he seemed immune to her charms.

"Do you know how to find the French Embassy?" He faced her.

Mouth open, she glanced around and then back at him. "Well, no, not exactly. But I know there is one. My parents just relocated here for international business arbitration. We dined at the embassy last night. The ambassador was charming." Boasting wasn't going to impress Andrew, but it did bolster her courage.

"You haven't changed." He grinned and shook his head. "I'm glad to see you're feeling better. Now let me find out how to take you where you belong. Let's hope it doesn't get me sent home." He continued speaking with the other missionary.

There wasn't much she could say to that. But it pleased her he was willing to risk his precious mission to help. Of course, she preferred not to need assistance.

She wanted Andrew to choose to be with her. However, she'd take whatever he offered at this point. Pain welled inside her and the hardest part was how familiar it felt.

When he faced her, she recognized something surprising in his expression. He felt the same way. They paused to look into the other's eyes.

She broke contact first, knowing he wanted to share his religion most of all. Religion had always come before anything else for him. Resentment hardened within her. His religion divided them, it always had. She hated it, The Church of Jesus Christ of Latter-day Saints.

Her mother had once called it heresy. Why would he choose heresy over her? The thought made her blood boil and her heart freeze at the same time.

"You can stay here forever for all I care," she said.

His expression softened and his eyes twinkled.

"I'll be home in six months. I hope you'll make time to talk to me then. It's good to see you, Nicole."

She looked him in the eyes and her anger melted. "I won't be in the States six months from now. I've been accepted at the Sorbonne in Paris."

"Graduate studies already? I only have a semester at UCLA."

"I don't waste time." She regretted saying that.

He frowned. "I'm not wasting time, Nicole."

"Regardless, Father says I'll make a great diplomat. I'm not so sure. But it's something I'm familiar with." She chewed her lip.

Now or never. "Join me. My apartment is big enough for two." It took everything she had to make this offer and the only reason she stopped short of asking him to marry her was that she knew he would insist on it.

His brows went up and then crashed into an expression of concern. "Nicole..." His lower lip trembled.

His cheeks grew rosy, but the rest of his face paled. He took a deep breath and looked at his hands. Gently shaking his head back and forth, his facial muscles tensed.

"I'm sorry. I can't."

Hot tears burst over her dark lashes to trace her face. She tilted her head to one side as she looked in sorrow at his unyielding expression. Her hand moved of its own accord to slap him squarely. The sound resounded in the subway car.

In apparent shock, the passengers forgot to look away. The other missionary scowled. Andrew slowly ducked his head and faced the firmly closed doors of the subway car.

Chapter Three

Andrew and his Korean missionary companion, Elder Lee HoJin, stood on the sidewalk in front of the French embassy. They watched Nicole Moreau's haughty figure stride through the gates. She wore Andrew's cardigan and scarf, causing him to shiver in the icy wind despite his coat and suitcoat. She didn't look back.

"I texted President Jones." Elder Lee's expression and tone conveyed his condolences regarding Nicole.

Andrew nodded and patted Elder Lee on the shoulder in thanks for his understanding. Andrew couldn't speak past the lump in his throat. Nicole had always been such a passionate person. She'd come all this way to throw herself at him. His hands trembled.

He wanted to run after her and make some kind of promise. He needed to tell her he loved her. If she'd only wait for him, then he would marry her in any church she chose. Thoughts of their future children stopped him. Nicole hated his religion, though he had no idea why.

He rubbed his face with both hands. He loved the Gospel of Jesus Christ. He couldn't turn his back on God. But Nicole needed him. For once in his life, he had no idea how to sort this out or make any kind of decision about what to do.

"There's the president's car." Elder Lee trotted along the busy sidewalk to the intersection so they could cross four lanes of traffic.

Andrew met his companion's determined expression. A feeling of guilt descended like a weight. Elder Lee nodded. Without a word, the two missionaries crossed the street and climbed into the back seat.

"President Jones, I can explain." Andrew wasn't positive he could.

"Have you Elders had anything to eat?" President's reassuring voice and the car's warmth soothed Andrew's fears.

Elder Lee shook his head. "Not in a while."

President Jones passed a candy bar to each of them.

"President, we helped a lost French woman. I have to tell you something. She's a friend of mine. She came from California to see me. I'm kind of shook up." Andrew's voice quavered.

Elder Lee ripped open the Free Time chocolate bar and took a bite, politely pretending not to hear the private conversation.

"So, what happened?" President turned to face the back seat.

Tears piqued in Andrew's eyes, and he leaned against the headrest. "My friend isn't a member of the church. She doesn't understand about serving a mission. I explained it when I left, but she just misses me too much, I guess.

"She found me at Jamshil Station by Lotte World. We were caught in a subway strike. The crowd crammed us like sardines into a subway car. Nicole and I were...close. She asked me to move to Paris with her. I said no. She slapped me." Andrew swiped at his eyes.

"She's in love with you?" President asked.

"I never thought so, but I've loved her since we were kids." Andrew took a tremulous breath.

"Elder, you've served an honorable mission for a year and a half. After twelve months, you can go home for any reason you choose."

"I didn't know that, President." The news was a shock.

"You need to decide what you should do. Pray about it and let me know. We can't stay parked here any longer." President pulled out into the congested Seoul traffic like a pro.

Andrew tried not to think about the advice. He loved being a missionary. But his focus was shattered. Something about what Nicole had asked, the look in her eyes and the little twitch in her cheek after she slapped him, said she needed him now.

"President, will you take me back to the embassy? I need to talk to her. I'm worried." A sense of urgency had built inside him.

"Calm down. Say a prayer. I'm driving back." President maneuvered through a rush of cars, trucks, and busses to turn right.

Andrew folded his arms in prayer. Why hadn't he realized when he had the chance just how out of character it was for Nicole to come here and make that offer? It was desperate and wasn't like her.

"I should have written her more letters." Andrew shook his head.

"We're here, Elder," President said.

Andrew jumped from the car and ran through the gates only to be stopped by two armed soldiers. "The French woman who came in a while ago. Where is she?"

"A car came for her a moment ago." The soldier spoke English with a thick French accent.

Andrew's heart sank. Nicole was gone, and he had no way to find her. With halting steps, he walked toward President's car. He was too late.

Chapter Four

M arina Moreau glanced at the text message on her phone. She stood from where she'd been working at her desk and walked toward the elevator, pushing the button. Concerned, she responded to Bertrand's warning.

After half a lifetime of cat and mouse with a North Korean assassin, her cover as a French Intelligence agent had been blown. Not just her identity, but her family's as well. Nicole was in danger.

Bertrand waited with the Rolls Royce at the curb.

She sat in the back seat. "Where is my daughter?"

He cleared his throat, avoiding her gaze in the rearview mirror. "She's with Andrew." He pulled out into the congested lanes of traffic.

A different kind of anger surged inside her. It was considerably warmer than the cold hatred she'd been experiencing for the past twenty-three years. It only happened when Nicole lost perspective with the gardener's son. The boy would never amount to anything, and neither would the relationship. She had determined long ago to do everything in her power to ensure that.

"She wouldn't say why she wanted to see him?" Morena thought about lighting a cigarette, but she'd quit.

Bertrand's expression closed up. "I think she's unhappy without him. You read her diary, so you tell me."

Marina smirked. "She's an open book, but...there's something she's not saying."

Bertrand scoffed.

Marina laughed with a dark edge. She was the one to keep secrets, not her daughter. She sighed, but it was more like exhaling a drag from a cigarette. Old habits.

"How did he find me? Do you think it was that last inquiry I made through the embassy last night at dinner?" Someone had leaked.

"I think the gunshot in Hong Kong inspired this level of scrutiny." Bertrand maneuvered to park at the curb at the French Embassy.

Marina laughed outright with wicked satisfaction. "He didn't need that kidney."

She would have ended the man and thought she had until he turned up again. Her aim had been knocked askew by one of the man's masked lackeys. It was irksome that she didn't know any of their real names, especially after this many years of effort in pursuit of answers.

She exited the Rolls and walked her high heels past the guards at the gate.

Nicole ran out to meet her.

Relief washed over Marina as she held her daughter in her arms. "What has happened?" The closeness became uncomfortable and she took a step backward.

Nicole only shook her head and wept.

Marina stroked her hair. "It will be all right again soon. Come. Bertrand is waiting."

The assassin would pay with his life this time. Bertrand had reported the incident with the canister. It had been a fortunate accident when Nicole had opened the car door and caused the assassin to lose control of the grenade before he'd pulled the pin.

Bertrand came around to open the door for them.

Nicole slid across the seat, picking up a small box off the floor mat. Marina sat beside her. Bertrand drove them to safety.

"What's that?" Infuriated, Marina had her suspicions.

"An early Christmas present for Andrew." Nicole choked up.

"You proposed marriage to that imbecile?" Blood pounded in Marina's temples.

"No. Well, I wanted to, but I misplaced the ring. I asked him to live with me in Paris." Tears fell down Nicole's cheeks behind a curtain of dark hair.

"Over my dead body! I still control your trust fund until you turn twenty-one in May and I forbid it." The need for a cigarette increased. She searched her clutch in vain.

"It doesn't matter now, anyway." Ugly crying ensued.

Marina handed a lace handkerchief to her daughter. "What happened, little one?"

Nicole dried her eyes and blew her nose, though it didn't stop the tears. "He said no. He doesn't love me, Maman."

"Thank God."

Marina leaned back in the leather seat, relaxing. Just then she noticed Andrew in a passing car. He looked distressed yet determined.

Marina glanced at Nicole, but she hadn't seen Andrew returning to the embassy. He'd come back for her daughter. Well, he was too late. Triumphant, she vowed that neither Andrew nor the North Korean agents who hunted Nicole would ever find her again.

Chapter Five

Nicole had the worst Christmas of her life with her parents. They gave her an unlimited line of credit at Harrod's in London. They arranged to have her fly back to South Korea for spring break to spend it with them on Jeju Island. Furthermore, they promised her a Porche in her choice of color for graduation, if only she would stay away from Andrew.

Unable to agree to the terms, she spent the day crying in her room. Andrew had said he wanted to see her in six months. How could he be content to wait that long? She was miserable without him.

The soonest flight she could book to California was for the day after Christmas. She eagerly took the early morning flight, wanting nothing more than to return to a sense of normalcy. Due to having crossed the international dateline, she arrived thirty-six hours later on the same day.

Mother had been concerned enough that she'd sent Bertrand along so Nicole wouldn't be alone. He'd been seated in coach. They disembarked at Los Angeles International Airport. Already tipsy from the alcohol she had flirted from the man sitting next to her in first class, she sent Bertrand to baggage claim. Then, she headed straight for the closest airport bar. It would be the last place Bertrand would look for her.

She entered the dim establishment with a determined stride. Pulling a hundred-dollar bill from her purse, she stood it curved on the bar seductively. The bartender caught sight of it right away.

"Margarita, barkeep."

She spoke perfect West Coast English but purposely laid on a heavy French accent. She laughed at the bartender's expression and sat on a barstool. He eyed her for a moment, but then nodded and made the drink.

She'd never had a margarita before but hardly tasted it after the hard liquor on the airplane. When she had finished the margarita, she caught the bartender's eye again.

"Would you like anything else?" His black slacks and wrinkled, red, silk shirt failed to pull off any sophistication.

She couldn't keep a straight face but kept up the accent. If only she were a few months older, then she wouldn't need to try this hard. However, she wasn't of legal drinking age yet, so she maintained the charade.

"Jack Daniels neat."

She had never cared to try American liquor. But when drowning the memory of an alcohol shunning Californian serving a mission in Asia, she found it fitting. Her forced mirth slipped at the thought of Andrew.

She quickly righted her expression and her thoughts as well. She needed to forget him. This would do the trick. She bolted the burning liquid and with watering eyes tapped the glass for another.

The bartender obliged. She relaxed on the bar stool as her vision blurred and her senses slowed. Oddly, the only thing left in her mind was Andrew. She had been in his arms, breathed the same air, touched his face, and slapped him.

A dark and dreamy stranger sat beside her. With a nod to the bartender, he held up two fingers. The bartender finished serving a drink to a patron down the bar. He then poured JD for her and the man beside her. The stranger smiled as she downed the shot.

"Are you on vacation?" He spoke English with an Asian accent.

"Something like that. I just flew in." She flashed her most charming smile even as the words slurred.

He grinned with perfect teeth. "May I take you to dinner? I know a beautiful Chinese restaurant not far from here." He slid closer.

"Take me to whatever restaurant you like." She staggered as she stood from the barstool. It was the last thing she remembered.

THE HARSH CLICK OF a hotel door as it closed awoke Nicole. It was a familiar sound because she traveled often. The light of morning entered the room through a gap in the curtains.

She squeezed her eyes shut. Her head pounded like a passenger train with all the cars empty. Where was she?

She closed her mouth only to find it parched and gritty. She'd been mouth breathing. Flat on her back and naked, she moved beneath the sheets of an unfamiliar bed.

Opening her eyes with a start, she winced at the pain in her most intimate place. She fought through dizziness to discover a man beside her. Sound asleep and snoring, all she could see was the back of his head and the bare contours of his body down to the cleft in his backside.

She had most of the covers.

Aching in ways she'd never hurt before, she fought her mortification and slid out of bed in search of clothes. Slipping into her underwear and fastening her bra, she noticed the bloodstain on the sheets where she had lain. Her expression darkened. She'd lost her virginity and didn't even know if she'd enjoyed it. Nauseous, she knew she hadn't.

It wasn't even a nice hotel.

Grim determination abandoned her, however, and her heart raced as the room spun. She caught her balance on the dresser along the wall and finished dressing. Purse. Smartphone. She snapped a couple of pictures of the sleeping man.

Headed for the door, she stumbled on his pants. A wallet fell from the back pocket. She stooped, flipped it open, and took another picture of the ID card. Dave Park age forty-three.

Her skin crawled as she considered the sexually transmitted diseases she might have acquired. Panic set in at the thought. Desperate, she searched for a condom wrapper either on the floor, the bedside table, in the trash, or even under the bed. She found none.

The man stirred before her as she held up the dust ruffle on the bed and stared at the board along the edge. He hadn't used protection. She looked at his face, noticing a mole on his forehead, his crooked nose, and his bad breath. He kept snoring. She dropped the dust ruffle and bolted out the door.

Even being peripherally Catholic, she had tried to be a good girl. She had flirted with a string of boyfriends, not because they interested her, but to make Andrew jealous. She had never gone all the way with any of them. She'd never wanted to. What if she became pregnant? Cold panic washed over her like a bucket of ice water.

"I need a taxi." She spoke to the attendant at the front desk.

"Right away." The man picked up the phone and ordered a car.

Nicole avoided his gaze. Still a little unsteady on her feet, she crossed the lobby and went outside to wait. The city smelled of exhaust and garbage. She clutched her jacket closed at the neck and watched for the cab. As it pulled up, she jerked the door open. Before the door shut, she called out the destination.

"Take me to the nearest hospital." She needed a terrible American invention, the morning after pill.

Her gorge threatened to rise, but she hugged herself tightly and watched the people walking on the streets as she rode past. How many Hail Mary's would it take to undo this? Since she'd never committed a major sin and had only gone to church with Mother at Christmas or Easter, she had no idea. Somehow, it didn't feel like it would work anyway.

Chapter Six

Two days after Christmas, Andrew took a plane home. Honorably released from his mission, he soon met with the Stake President of his home Stake in L.A. After that, he changed out of his mission suit into jeans and a nice shirt. It felt weird to wear casual clothes again.

His parents looked worried. He'd explained the situation, but they had simply gone quiet. He had chosen Nicole.

He drove to the nearest jeweler and spent an hour selecting the best-looking ring he could buy with the pathetically small amount of money he had. He knew her size. He'd known since they were sixteen.

He wished he'd talked to her about how he felt. He wished things were different. Worry made him lengthen his stride and quicken his steps. Even so, he couldn't shake the haunting feeling of dread.

He drove his dad's old truck to the Moreau's mansion, arriving as a taxi excited and the gates closed. The estate sprawled before him. He cranked down the window and pressed the button on the box in the driveway to page the house. His heart beat as though it would crash through his chest.

"Moreau residence," Bertrand's voice stated.

"Bertrand, I need to see Nicole. Please, let me in."

Silence prevailed for several minutes.

"She says, no." Bertrand's tone projected from the speaker tight and protective, leaving no room for argument.

Andrew pushed the button again. No one answered. He looked

across the lawn at the house. The curtains in Nicole's bedroom moved. She was watching him.

He jumped from the silver truck and waved both arms high in the air. The curtain closed. He walked up and shook the gates, but they didn't budge.

Andrew sat in the truck watching the house for an hour, but the curtains remained still. He pushed the button, but again no one answered. Unable to sit still any longer, he paced along the tall, wrought-iron fence.

He had to see her. Something wasn't right. He bowed his head in prayer and felt like he knew what he must do. He climbed the fence and strode across the lawn.

The door opened. Nicole's silhouette stood in the entryway. Two guard dogs growled at her side.

"Don't come any closer, Andrew." She stepped backward, shrinking from the light.

She looked drawn as if she hadn't slept in days. He ran toward her.

"Please, Nicole, talk to me."

She unleashed the dogs.

"Attack."

Chapter Seven

Marina Moreau pulled up to the L.A. house in a hired limo direct from the airport just as an ambulance drove from the opposite side of the circle. Bertrand was covered in blood from hands to elbows with spatters across the rest of him. She flew from the car to his side.

"Is Nicole alive?" Like a repeated prayer, her heart pounded against the crucifix on her chest.

"She's inside. The dogs attacked Andrew. It's serious." Bertrand stood beside two police officers.

"The boy's a stalker. Why was he trespassing?" She steered suspicion away from Nicole.

"Who set the dogs on him?" The officer with a tablet asked.

Bertrand looked stricken. "No one. They roam the grounds night and day. To be honest, they're friendly dogs. I have no idea what the young man did to deserve such an attack. He wasn't welcome here, but I would never wish him harm."

"Who are you, Ma'am?" the officer asked.

Marina straightened her posture. "I own this house and just arrived home from the airport."

"Your daughter is Nicole Moreau?" he asked.

"Yes. Is she all right? I saw the blood and thought the worst. This stalker business has me on edge." She was throwing Andrew under the bus, exactly where he deserved to be.

"She's fine. She was asleep upstairs." He scratched his head, quirked an eyebrow, and looked Marina in the eyes. "I may have more questions. None of you should leave town until the matter is settled."

Idiot. "Of course." She faced Bertrand. "Is any of that blood yours?" He shook his head.

"Then clean up while I see to Nicole."

"Is this your husband, Ma'am?"

She leveled a severe expression on the man. "He is our chauffeur."

"Shouldn't he have picked you up at the airport?"

"It's his day off."

The officer tipped his cap at her. "Right."

Annoyed, Marina went into the house and up to Nicole's room. Lightly knocking, she proceeded into the spacious room. The vestments of her daughter's personal effects had long ago been moved to her college dorm room at Berkeley. The things that remained were childish keepsakes that would soon be packed for shipping to Korea by the servants.

"Nicole? Where are you?" Marina walked into the large bathroom.

The muffled sound of someone crying came from behind the walk-in shower door. "Mother?"

"I'm here."

Marina's heart quailed. Of all the situations she'd been in over the years, this was by far the most terrifying. Her child was in pain.

"Is Andrew okay?"

With a sigh and without looking, Marina handed Nicole a monogrammed robe. "Come out of there."

Nicole obeyed. "I set the dogs on him. Why would I do that?"

Marina had to think fast. Over the last couple of hours, Bertrand had been filling her in by text as information came to light. Nicole had been drugged and sexually assaulted.

Bertrand had sent her the pictures on Nicole's phone. Dave Park was an alias for the Medusa. Surveillance video from the hotel had been troubling, to say the least. If she thought about it too much just now, then she wouldn't be of help to her daughter.

"You did what you needed to do. Andrew was angry because he was sent home early from his mission. He'll get over it. I saw him, he's going to be fine. I expect he will call to apologize any time now." Marina guided Nicole to the bed and turned back the coverlet.

"Maman, I did something terrible. Unforgivable." Nicole shivered and her hair dripped with water from the shower.

"Non, ma petite. All is well. You did nothing wrong." Marina dried Nicole's hair with a towel and then tucked her child into bed.

"I drank too much and slept with a stranger. Andrew will never forgive me." Nicole's eyelids drooped even as the tension in the corners intensified and her pulse visibly throbbed in her temples.

"A boy like that may not forgive, but I do not blame you. Rest, little one." Marina would avenge her daughter's violation and take exquisite delight in doing so.

"Don't leave me." Nicole reached out to her.

"I'll stay awhile, but you must sleep." She sat on the bed's edge and caressed her daughter's weary face.

"Are you sure he's all right?" Nicole's voice trailed off into slumber.

"Yes, not a scratch." Marina felt no remorse about lying.

Dark thoughts curled inside her mind. She planned cruel methods for the Medusa's demise. No level of brutality would be enough to satisfy her hatred.

Chapter Eight

Andrew awoke from a painkiller-induced slumber. He'd spent the night in the hospital under observation after being mauled by Nicole's attack dogs. He still couldn't believe she'd set them on him. Neither could he believe the dumb mutts had bitten him, especially after all the bones he'd brought them over the years.

It had taken seventy-three stitches to put him back together. He would have some gnarly scars on his arms. Yet, the real hurt had come when Nicole didn't call off the dogs. She'd retreated inside the house, leaving Bertrand to pull them off and call an ambulance.

The single mercy was that she hadn't pressed trespassing charges. The dark thought that she might have twisted like a knife in his gut. One day she wanted to live with him and the next she wanted him chewed to pieces.

He adjusted his head on the pillow and breathed deeply through his nose to avoid crying. He didn't have a private room. The hospital staff came in and out regularly. The police had looked at him like some kind of criminal for jumping the fence. He wouldn't make that mistake twice. If Nicole ever wanted to see him again then she'd have to come to him.

He clenched his fists despite the pain it caused. She should have come to see him by now. Her anger had never been this implacable in the past. Of course, he guessed she'd never been hurt this badly before. Still, he expected flowers and a note, some kind of apology, but nothing came.

His parents walked into the room. He could see their tennis shoes under the privacy curtain around his bed. They parted the curtain, walked in, and let it fall closed. The look on his father's face and the concern etched around his mother's eyes told Andrew something far more disturbing than his situation had gone wrong.

"What is it?" His stomach did a flip-flop.

"Your Grams just called and Grandpa Joe passed away this morning." Mom had been crying.

Every thought in his mind went blank and his heart went thud as if it would never start again. "A letter came from Grandpa last week. He seemed fine. Did he know I came home early?"

Andrew's dad shook his head. He sniffled and wiped the tears off his face. Mom handed him a handkerchief from her purse.

"No, he didn't know. Don't blame yourself. He had a heart attack on the mesa. Grams saw him fall in the hayfield. By the time she helped him into the truck and drove him down the mountain, he had passed away. She was beside herself on the phone, but she did say he always wanted to go out working." She hugged dad and then came over to hold Andrew's hand.

He didn't try to withhold his tears this time. They wept together for a while until the question came to him. "What will Grams do with the ranch?"

"She's going to sell." Dad nodded grimly. "The family is in no position to run it. We've all chosen different lives. She can't afford to hire someone because it no longer makes much of a profit. Times have changed for ranchers." His father shook his head. "Once it sells, she'll be able to live comfortably. She deserves that."

Andrew nodded his understanding even though he felt crushed by the prospect of not spending time on his grandparents' ranch. He'd spent two weeks there every summer break since he could remember, bringing in the hay and horseback riding. It was his favorite place on earth. He would miss it.

"How long do you think it will take to sell?" A million memories of grandpa ran through his head.

"That's the problem. It could take years. The market is still down." His father shook his head. "She asked for your help, Andrew."

Andrew met his father's gaze and eventually nodded his understanding. It was the right thing to do. Besides, it would keep him out of trouble for a while.

"I'll go, but if Nicole comes looking for me, I expect you to tell her where I am."

His parents nodded. "We will, son."

Chapter Nine

Two years passed quickly at the Sorbonne. Nicole's studies consumed her days and often her nights as she earned her master's degree. She considered it unpleasantly American to be this lopsided. As a French woman, she should know how to enjoy life far better.

Her thoughts were bitter and today's graduation ceremony felt somehow hollow. Her parents could not attend. Father had phoned to say they were dealing with a business crisis in Seoul. His voice had been so full of tension that she didn't complain. They were arbitrating a dispute between mainland China and a Korean electronics manufacturer.

Grand-mere had planned to attend the graduation. Sadly, she had been in Tuscany on one of her buying trips and her flight to Paris was delayed by weather. Nicole had no other relatives to celebrate the day with, only friends from her tightknit graduating class. Unfortunately for Nicole, they all had families of their own to satisfy.

During the speeches, she had time to reflect on her future. With three offers on the table for nice positions within the French government, she was pleased. Her only hesitation in accepting one of them was a desire to obtain her parents' advice.

Despite everything she had done to build a life here, her heart wasn't in Paris. She simply couldn't forget Andrew. Many things reminded her of him.

Pleasant memories mingled with hurt as she thought of how

affronted he'd been when she'd slapped him in the subway car so long ago. That's when they had turned from each other. She hadn't found a way back to him, or an opportunity to fix anything. Not after she'd blacked out drunk and slept with someone else.

Regardless, she wished Andrew could somehow be a part of this day. He would be proud of her accomplishments. Well, perhaps not.

She was certain he must hate her after being mauled by Yar and Worf. She no longer understood the calloused way she had set her father's Dobermans on him. At the time, it had seemed the only means of defense. She'd felt justified. Now, it seemed unnecessarily cruel.

She couldn't expect forgiveness.

The dean called out names. Ahead of her, the students filed forward to receive their degrees. She followed in turn. Exaggerated smiles and the flash of cameras did nothing to lift her spirits.

Something nagged at the corners of her mind. Why had her father said he loved her? To some, the answer might be obvious. But the easy answer was incorrect.

Father seldom shared his feelings with her because he was a private man. But he had a pet name for her that always let her know he adored her. He called her his little Klingon since she'd been his shadow from the time she could walk.

His generosity was matched only by his high expectations. Even so, he had never lavished her with words of love. She could not remember a single time since she was little that he had told her he loved her.

The dean called her name. She went through the motions of receiving her diploma. She even smiled for the photographers. Her photo would be on the society page of tomorrow's paper, so she made it good. But her mind returned to her worries when she resumed her seat.

The smartphone clipped to her waistband under her robe vibrated. Regrettably, she couldn't reach it now. In rapid succession, it vibrated several more times before the ceremony ended. What could be so important?

Avoiding the smiling families and beaming graduates, she hurried to the lounge. She had hoped in vain that it would not be crowded. At least she was able to remove her gown to access her phone.

Five voice messages waited for her.

She left the lounge and entered an empty room along a corridor. After listening to the first voicemail from her mother, she collapsed to her knees. Her father had died.

Mother sobbed, saying she would have more information soon. In the next message, she explained that the South Korean police had ruled it a suicide. She said not to believe it. Their business arbitration had failed, but he would never kill himself.

Nicole played the last three messages. Two contained increasing levels of hysterics. Her mother sounded unwell. The last was from Bertrand and said they were boarding a plane for Paris.

Nicole couldn't move. The shock made her feel faint, but she didn't heed the danger. Her trembling hands dropped the phone. Unable to face the news, she curled into a ball on the floor.

Chapter Ten

Nicole had found her way home and slept a little, but the strain of her father's death weighed heavily. Bertrand was traveling with Mother and had sent their itinerary in a text message. Nicole made sure she was there to meet the plane on time and parked her BMW in the parking garage. Needing her mother, she hurried to the security checkpoint inside the airport.

Emergency personnel raced past her. Their gurney landed a careless blow to her left elbow. Throbbing in agony, she rubbed it. She watched them rush past security and down the airy corridor to the terminals.

Not more than two minutes later, the emergency medical personnel hustled her way again. This time, Bertrand was right beside the person on the gurney. His face appeared drawn and exhausted. The EMT's passed through the security checkpoint.

Nicole's heart pounded when she realized the unconscious person on the gurney was her mother. "What's the matter?"

"I thought she was sleeping but I couldn't wake her." Bertrand rubbed his face with one hand as he held Mother's hand with the other.

Nicole hurried along beside them.

The paramedics didn't stop, so there was no time for more answers. They loaded Mother into the ambulance. Bertrand ushered Nicole inside. She tossed her keys to him just before the doors slammed shut. The ambulance took off with lights and sirens, leaving Bertrand on the sidewalk.

"What's the matter with her?" Nicole had never seen her mother this pale.

The paramedic finished sliding in an intravenous line and pushed fluids. "It's hard to say. Acts like poisoning."

The shock made Nicole go numb. Was that how her father had died? Would she lose her mother too?

"Will she be all right?" Stars floated in Nicole's vision.

"She's being well taken care of." He kept working, never meeting Nicole's gaze.

The vehicle came to an abrupt stop and the back doors burst open. Mother was rushed inside a hospital emergency room. Nicole followed on unsteady legs.

"Wait here." A nurse waved her off before the gurney passed between two doors.

This couldn't be happening.

IN THE WEEK THAT FOLLOWED, Nicole's mother was transferred to a long-term care facility in Paris. She was heavily medicated and on kidney dialysis for poisoning. A medically induced coma had been implemented to expedite the healing process.

Each visit caused Nicole agony. The two of them had never had a close relationship. The idea they might never have the chance to develop one devastated her. She held her mother's hand almost around the clock.

"I love you." Nicole's voice came out a hoarse whisper from the seat beside the hospital bed.

Mother showed no sign of recognition, not of herself, her daughter, this horrible place, or the words that had been spoken. The doctors said Marina Moreau had suffered a physical setback that would take weeks of extensive therapy. That was if she survived at all.

Due to the scandal frenzied media, Nicole hadn't gone back to her apartment. Details were sketchy, but her parents' disgrace had been profound. The press splashed salacious headlines while the media hounded her for details.

She didn't have any answers for them. She'd asked Bertrand, but he didn't know anything.

Father was accused of everything from embezzlement to involvement with the CIA. She no longer blamed him for committing suicide. Her thoughts and emotions had sunk so low this past week that she almost envied his release from this life.

She squeezed her mother's limp hand.

Nicole was cut adrift from all she knew and loved. Her diligently sought future spread before her in smoking ruins. The three offers for employment had been rescinded. Even the private sector wanted nothing to do with the Moreau name. Her life was a burning building and she was trapped on the roof.

The family's bank accounts were frozen while investigators probed into her parents' business. There would be no more allowance. She only had a few thousand Euros and they wouldn't last long. Her friends declined to return her calls, and random strangers on the street spit in her direction.

The whole thing baffled her. Unfortunately, she had more questions than anyone. What had offended the Chinese government? How had her father committed suicide? When would the details be available? Why had his body been discovered in a whore house?

The crimson heat of profound embarrassment arose in her cheeks. Seeking comfort, she rubbed her mother's unresponsive hand. What depths of despair could have forced Father to kill himself?

"Oh, Maman, why would he do it?" Nicole hoped for a response but received only silence.

Chapter Eleven

A media maelstrom swirled around Nicole's family. Having fled her apartment with the onslaught of unwanted attention from the press, she now stood at a desk in a bedroom suite in her grandmother's Paris mansion. She used the landline to contact potential employers.

One by one, they refused to take her calls. Finding a job in the city proved close to impossible. The likelihood of finding one in France grew slimmer by the minute as speculation intensified and spread. Any hopes that the scandal would go away had been dashed.

Giving up for the day, Nicole trudged to the window. Through the sheer curtains, she watched the reporters outside the gates. Drones buzzed the yard, searching for a photo op.

She slipped deeper into depression.

Officials had visited her grandmother's house early this morning to interview both of them. That had been an unpleasant experience. The phone rang endlessly. Grand-mere said she couldn't stand much more.

Nicole needed to find a way to improve the situation. She walked to the desk. Not at all sure what to do, she reached for the phone out of reflex. Her heart contracted with pain to realize she had intended to call her father to ask for advice.

A knock came at the door.

"Yes?"

A gray outfitted servant entered the room carrying a fairly large package. "This just came for you, Mademoiselle."

Nicole nodded. "Put it here." She indicated the desktop.

The servant bowed and departed.

Korean lettering adorned the return address. An eerie feeling hollowed out the center of her chest. She pulled a box cutter from a desk drawer and sliced the box open.

Under an excessive amount of packing material, she found a metallic lid. She pulled a tall cylindrical object from the box. It wasn't overly heavy, but she nearly dropped it when she realized she held her father's urn.

They had sent him back from South Korea like this, without so much as a note. Instead of being devastated, as she suspected had been their intention, she grew angry. This could not stand.

This injustice would simmer until she found a way to clear her father's name. Somehow. Someday.

"I will make this right, papa."

THAT EVENING, NICOLE carried Father's urn into the facility where Mother received treatment. Bertrand had driven her. Two burly bodyguards now accompanied them anytime they left Grand-mere's mansion.

The nurse at the desk buzzed them all through the security doors. The woman eyed the urn but quickly returned to her computer, ignoring the group. Nicole walked the white corridor, nauseated by the sterile air and the glossy tile floor.

The door to Mother's room stood open. Nicole found that odd. Always, in the past few days, it had been closed.

As she entered, she found a shockingly familiar Asian man standing beside Mother's bed. He held a syringe at her neck. Startled, he glanced Nicole's way just before he would have plunged the needle into flesh.

Bertrand bumped into the back of Nicole.

The man with the syringe moved to finish his deed. Nicole threw the urn at his head. It hit with a resonant thud.

Amid the ash cloud, the man dropped the syringe and leaped over Mother's unconscious body to the other side of the bed. He brandished a gun. The bodyguards didn't have weapons.

The middle-aged Asian assassin lifted his chin, indicating that they should back out of the room.

Bertrand stepped in front of her. He shook his head at the man, maintaining eye contact. He pulled Nicole along behind him toward her mother's bedside.

"Let him out of the room," Bertrand spoke to the bodyguards.

The burly men obeyed.

With a sneer, the attacker dashed away.

Bertrand and the guards ran after him.

In the adrenaline-charged silence, Nicole checked her mother's breathing. She was fine. The syringe on the floor contained air. Nicole had seen enough television to know that this had been an assassination attempt.

Worse yet, she knew the man. It was Dave Park from her one-night-stand years ago. With trembling hands, she retrieved her father's spilled urn.

Beyond the point of shock, she fell to her knees. Why would that man be here to kill Mother? Had the one-night-stand been a setup? Who was he? She shook her head to clear it.

"Papa, you saved Maman's life." The thought occurred to her that if someone was indeed trying to kill her mother, her father may have saved her twice.

Chapter Twelve

Nicole passed a sleepless night in her suite at Grand-mere's. Early the next morning, a knock came at the bedroom door.

"I'm awake," she called.

A servant woman entered. "Madame Augustine would like you to come to tea."

Nicole frowned. Tea at this hour? "I'll be down shortly."

The servant bowed and closed the door.

Nicole knew the invitation wasn't for a simple chat, so she showered and dressed appropriately.

After she descended the stairs, she found Grand-mere in the parlor. The morning sun shone through the open drapes. The hum of drones gathering outside the windows increased. This meeting would be seen by the whole world.

Nicole approached the tea-table.

Elaina arose and took her hand. "Nicolette, you must not think I do not love you."

Nicole sighed and squeezed her grandmother's hand. "I know Grand-mere. I can't stay here any longer. But who knows when the account freezes will be lifted and everything settled with Mother's care, not to mention the family estate? I had hoped things would quiet but there's no telling when that might happen."

She chewed her bottom lip as she pulled out a chair and sat. Frustration and fear wrote ugly thoughts in her heart.

Grand-mere nodded and poured the fragrant tea. "I have made sure Marina will be cared for. It's you I'm worried about. It appears that even when your finances are settled, your life will never be easy in Paris."

Nicole glanced at the drones.

"Sharon, please close the drapes." Grand-mere's command was obeyed by the long-time family servant attending the tea.

"I hope you don't mind but I took the liberty of arranging a diversion for you. A little trip. But before you leave, I want you to have this." A white box tied with a blue ribbon sat between them on the table. The older woman leaned forward and picked it up.

Nicole's brows creased in the middle because Grand-mere's tone indicated she wasn't sure the gift would be appreciated.

"Please, I—"

Elaina Augustine held up one hand and proffered the box with the other. "Just look at it." Her eyes held a reassuring sparkle.

Nicole bowed her head. "Of course, thank you, Grand-mere." She pulled the ribbon and opened the box. Inside the folds of white tissue paper, she found a large gold crucifix on a heavy chain.

"Marina would want you to have it." Grand-mere sipped her tea.

The declaration sounded final. Until this moment, Nicole had dared to hope her mother would recover. But now, faced with this, she doubted. Panic clawed at the inside of her chest.

"Look beneath the necklace. You will find documents to aid you in the task I've set. You need a plan. I believe this one suits the occasion and your temperament."

Beneath the crucifix lay Nicole's passport and documents detailing a real-estate search for a rural property in the United States. Her eyes widened as her gaze flew to meet her grandmother's.

"You're sending me away?" Nicole had intended to leave to spare Grand-mere's peace of mind, but she had not anticipated being rejected.

"Yes, to find a suitable place for your mother to convalesce. You know how much she avoids Paris, although I suspect she never told you why."

Nicole lifted her eyebrows in question.

The older woman shook her head. "I will authorize the funds you need. I'm sure you will enjoy this corner of the world, considering your interest in photography. As far as I can tell, there is no more noteworthy place to photograph. No one will recognize you there. You will travel in my jet and be quite anonymous."

Nicole's eyes filled with tears. It was all too much.

"Now, now, don't cry." Grand-mere smiled. "I didn't give you the crucifix for any other purpose except to remind you that you have a responsibility toward your mother. I hope you don't read anything more into it.

"Marina may be Catholic, but I'm Protestant. You, my dear, may choose to be anything you wish, although I hope you don't follow in your father's atheist footprints."

She squeezed Nicole's hand. "I'm saying you should take the time to reflect on the meaning of life. Enjoy the beauties of this earth without the pressure of society, me, or anyone else." The older woman's eyes remained concerned and tinged with sadness.

Nicole looked at the cross and the information beneath it in the box. She needed to go. "You're right, Grand-mere. I will find a good place for Mother. She was happiest in America. Thank you." She forced a pleasant expression and stood. "I'll pack my things."

"Everything you need is already in the car. The jet is waiting. Bon voyage, ma chouchoute."

Chapter Thirteen

Nicole fell asleep on the flight from Paris to Moab. Bertrand awoke her with a touch on the arm as they landed. Why had Grand-mere chosen Utah?

The enormous crucifix hanging from her neck weighed heavily. She tucked it inside her blouse and reminded herself she was not her mother. She needed to purchase a quiet place in the world where she too could be happy.

Her mother needed seclusion to remain safe. Unfortunately, so did Nicole. At that moment, the whole thing felt like exile. Could her future have evaporated?

Grand-mere knew all of Nicole's secrets. They had been confidants throughout Nicole's life, mostly because she had no one else to turn to. Even so, trusting her grandmother now proved challenging. Did the older woman have an ulterior motive?

"Your car awaits, Mademoiselle." Bertrand wore the gray uniform with black buttons and trim of Grand-mere's household.

Nicole regretted not having Bertrand on her parents' payroll anymore but at least he was still with her. She didn't know what she would do without him. He'd been there for her all her life until he had relocated with her parents to Seoul.

"Thank you, Bertrand." She gathered a handbag and a smartphone.

She'd been forced to accept a burner and ditch her old phone because someone had hacked it. The proof had been the use of personal photos splashed across the media. What had hurt the most was the use of the hysterical messages Mother had left regarding Father's death. She hadn't erased them because it was the last time her mother had spoken to her and she missed the sound of her voice.

Bertrand gave Nicole a look of concern. She tried to quit scowling. He took instructions from Grand-mere now. That felt strange. Nicole herself felt like nothing more than an extension of the older woman's hand. She would pay Grand-mere back when the investigation concluded...once it was proven that her father hadn't been guilty of embezzlement.

Nicole sighed deeply. Regardless, she trusted Grand-mere's taste and judgment. After all, this is what the woman had done all her life, negotiate international property deals. It was why Mother loved traveling so much. She'd grown up in exotic locales.

The leer jet came to rest on the tarmac. The sudden lack of movement drew Nicole's attention. The door opened. Hot, dry air sucked the climate-controlled atmosphere from the plane.

They proceeded through security at the tiny airport and walked to the parking lot. A black SUV pulled around. Bertrand took the keys from a rustic looking man. He gave the vehicle a thorough once over and then ushered her into the back seat.

He loaded the luggage and then drove through red sandstone canyons. They passed the entrance to Arches National Park, and Nicole rubbernecked to see what that was about. But there wasn't much visible from the highway.

They crossed the Colorado River and drove through the red rock valley that held the tourist town of Moab. Numerous hotels mingled with fossil shops, Jeep rental agencies, and restaurants. The architectural theme seemed to be red southwest intermixed with an eclectic blend of other facades. She found it tacky, yet somehow exhilarating.

She'd never seen any place like it. The main thoroughfare was packed with vehicles, and the sidewalks crowded with pedestrians of every shade, and if she were correct, every nationality.

"What do you know about Moab, Bertrand?" She had never been to such a small town in the States.

"It has a population of five thousand with tens of thousands of tourists from around the world visiting daily. It wasn't easy to secure these accommodations because everything was taken."

"What accommodations?"

"Madame Augustine has leased a house, Mademoiselle."

"She took a house just for a buying trip?" That seemed peculiar.

"It's more secure. She couldn't be sure you wouldn't be followed."

Bertrand turned the SUV onto a side street at the edge of town. They soon arrived at a gated community and a good-sized house with a circular drive. Bertrand parked and opened the SUV door for her.

Appraising the house, she decided she liked the modern architecture. Bertrand unlocked the front door, and she preceded him inside. In the entryway, she surveyed the lavish rooms open to view.

"Follow me, Mademoiselle." He carried her things as he led her to the second story bedrooms.

The furniture was passable, though not the trendy colors she preferred, or the antiques Grand-mere adored. With a sigh, she knew her tastes would have to adjust. Life had changed.

An oppressive cloud fell over her. It often had since she received the news of Father's death. Thoughts of his urn, packed in a plain box and shipped from South Korea without ceremony, ran through her mind.

Mother would have had an open casket funeral with a graveside service. It probably would have rained. That seemed fitting. She would have bought him a casket like the one in his favorite science-fiction show. His eulogy would have been light, even humorous, something about living long and prospering.

The truth sunk in. Mother would have wanted a Catholic burial. Certainly, the church would not have accepted an atheist believed to have committed suicide. The pain of that would have devastated her mother.

Furthermore, the scandal frenzied media would have ruined everything with intrusions and camera flashes. That was only the beginning. No one beside herself would have dared to attend except Mother, Grand-mere, and Bertrand.

Perhaps, it was for the best they hadn't gone through that. It didn't feel better, however. She hadn't had a chance to grieve properly...if there was such a thing.

Glancing around the wide, impersonal bedroom of her temporary home, she realized she hadn't cried yet.

Bertrand left the suitcases in the walk-in closet and went down for more. At the heart of the room lay a California king size bed. Her petite frame would hardly be noticeable when lying in it.

Grand-mere often repeated the phrase, 'you need a husband, Nicolette.' But after the utter fool Nicole had made of herself with Andrew and the colossal mistake she'd made with Dave Park directly thereafter, she had stayed clear of men. Grand-mere had asked if she swung the other way, but that wasn't it. Nicole had simply believed she had more time, that is until time ended. Now she was caught with no one to console her when she needed someone.

Bertrand walked into the room with more suitcases and a tall redhead in tow. The young woman proceeded to unpack Nicole's suitcases.

"Would you like to see the rest of the house, Mademoiselle?" Bertrand's expression quirked with amusement, probably because she was glowering at the new servant.

She took the hint and allowed the servant to do her job. "Thank you, no, Bertrand. Please, have dinner brought up. I'll be on the balcony."

She walked out the double doors to take in the view of cottonwood trees and a creek at the bottom of the yard. Other houses surrounded them, but not as close as in Paris. She sat on a patio chair and breathed in the unique smell of dry, clean air.

Without warning, a sprinkling of rain fell. It stirred up a layer of red dust that coated everything outdoors. With it came the most heavenly fragrance she'd ever encountered. She breathed deeply as the rain fell in earnest for an instant and then quit altogether. The sun shone through the clouds to cook off the brief reprieve from the intense desert heat.

She dried the water droplets on her sunglasses with her black blouse. She'd have to rethink her wardrobe, or at least make accommodations for lighter colors. The dark shades of mourning weren't practical here. Father wouldn't mind. Even so, it felt like a betrayal.

The redheaded servant brought out a dinner tray. She was dressed in the uniform of Grand-mere's household, but this woman could not be French. She nodded to Nicole.

"Tell me your name," Nicole spoke in English, though she deliberately took no care to eliminate her French accent. She could speak without it, but maintaining a barrier with the help felt more comfortable at the moment.

"Athena Westwood, Mademoiselle." She spoke the word well.

"Do you speak French, Athena?" Nicole raised an eyebrow, dubious.

"Not well, Mademoiselle. Not like a native. I took this job in hopes of maintaining my language skills and expanding my vocabulary." She spoke all of it in fluent French.

Nicole waved her hand as Athena proffered the bottle of wine she'd brought with the dinner tray. "Then speak it as you wish."

The young woman bowed, put the bottle on ice, and backed away.

"Are you a Mormon, Athena?"

Nicole's suspicions had been aroused by some nuance of expression Athena had shown concerning the wine. Though, perhaps it was the presence of the wine at all because Nicole didn't drink often. Why then had Bertrand ordered alcohol sent up now?

"I served eighteen months in France as a missionary for the Church of Jesus Christ of Latter-day Saints, Mademoiselle." Athena beamed. Her accent was nearly flawless.

"You have no problem offering me alcohol?"

Athena flushed a rather lovely shade of pink, like a Titian painting. Nicole missed the Louvre. Interestingly, seeing art and experiencing this moment were vastly different. She found herself enjoying this more.

"I hope you won't ask me to drink it or this will be the shortest job I hope to ever have." The casual declaration held neither affront nor condescension.

"Of course not." Nicole waved her hand.

Athena bowed and left.

Did all Mormons have this much self-assurance? It reminded her of Andrew. She looked at the cottonwood trees and focused on the clatter of leaves in the breeze. Thoughts of him drove her appetite away. She let her meal grow cold.

Had he married someone like Athena? He would be graduating from UCLA next spring if he'd been diligent. Had he stuck with Elementary Education or opted for something that would support a large family?

A little bird landed on the balcony railing. She pinched crust from her dinner roll and placed it nearby. The bird hopped forward, took the bread in its beak, and flew to a tree branch.

Needling herself with unhappy thoughts of Andrew married to someone else only worked so long to fend off the inevitable sense of longing, nostalgia, and need that followed thoughts of him. In times of idleness, her loneliness made her remember the feel of his hand in hers as they walked various L.A. parks as teenagers. A glimmer of joy upturned her lips to remember the way he served a tennis ball backhanded like he was playing badminton.

Unbidden, she remembered his pine fresh scent when she had laid her head on his chest during the subway strike in Seoul. Missing him terribly, tears came to her eyes. How could he have let her go just because she didn't belong to his church? Even now, she couldn't understand it.

With a heavy heart, she lifted Mother's crucifix from where it lay concealed beneath her blouse. The figure of God depicted on it was pathetic. Pitiable. Horrible. She didn't believe in a God whose suffering never ended, did she? There was no hope in such a God. Nicole needed hope more than anything.

Her father had been an atheist. So, despite Mother's wishes for her to attend Catholic school, Nicole received a secular education at a prestigious private school. Father had insisted.

Nicole had only attended Mass a few times in her life. Though the experience had been memorable, it hadn't inspired any real loyalty to the religion. She knew more about what Andrew believed than what her mother did, or what she herself believed for that matter. She shivered, uncomfortable with the thoughts.

She abandoned dinner and found her journal. Athena had placed it on the bedside table along with a pen. Nicole found that curious, but took up the pen and journal and lay on the bed to compose a list of her beliefs.

When finished, she looked over the list and concluded she must be Buddhist, except for the part about believing in the Buddha. With a sigh, she rolled onto her side and closed her journal watching the cottonwood leaves rustle outside the open doors. For the air conditioner's sake, she should have closed the doors, but she didn't care.

Chapter Fourteen

The next morning, Nicole stood by the window, checking her phone for the time. The realtor pulled to the curb twenty minutes late. She marched out to meet him.

Unfortunately, he insisted Nicole and Bertrand ride with him.

He navigated a minivan through town, hitting every pothole. The vehicle smelled of something distasteful like stale vomit and dog. The tropical scented, palm tree-shaped air freshener dangling from the rearview mirror increased her nausea as it swung back and forth.

Each property they stopped at seemed less worthy than the last. None of them approached the suitability of the house Grand-mere had leased, let alone rose to Nicole's standard. However, she found the prices of these houses astounding.

"How can most people live and work in Moab? It seems only the rich can afford a decent home." She spoke her thoughts out loud.

The realtor nodded. "Unless you inherit, that's about it," he said. "Most people make do the best they can. This next property is further out of town in Spanish Valley and it's larger. I hope you like it."

The realtor drove them along a two-lane road. They passed through a four-way stop and a kilometer later took a left. The road transitioned to dirt as it neared the valley's northern edge.

Without stepping foot from the vehicle, Nicole knew the place was too small. It was also too close to other houses. The realtor's enthusiasm and her own need to escape the stinky van encouraged her to take a look at it anyway. She discovered some features she enjoyed like a paved courtyard, but nothing that impressed her.

"Thank you for your help today. It seems that existing homes will not suit. Please, research property for our next outing. I'd like something with picturesque views and privacy." Nicole reluctantly returned to the van and the realtor drove her and Bertrand home.

IN THE COMFORT OF HER rooms, Nicole showered off the day's unpleasantness. Athena brought an early dinner. With her hair wrapped in a towel and a robe cinched around her waist, Nicole ate the savory meal in the bedroom's dining nook.

The servant scrubbed the shower, wiped counters, and gathered dirty laundry. Apparently, she hadn't learned to do those things when Nicole wasn't around. Yet today, the quiet efficiency of Athena's industry soothed Nicole's frayed nerves. Truth be told, she didn't want to be alone.

"Have you had supper?" She offered an excuse for the young woman to stay as she finished cleaning.

Athena carried the laundry toward the bedroom door. "No, Mademoiselle." She performed her trademark not at all subservient, though humble bow.

"I have questions about the area that need to be answered before I can proceed with my property search. Would you join me and answer them?" Nicole indicated the generous selection of food and the chair opposite her at the small table.

"I'd be happy to. I'll just take down the laundry and bring up a place setting." With carrot-colored tresses trailing behind her, she hurried downstairs and returned with the same enthusiasm.

Nicole wasn't sure what to think. In a normal situation, a servant dropped whatever they were doing and obeyed her wishes immediately. Athena's response wasn't disrespectful, nor did it seem like a welcome reprieve from the work, but instead it was a willing concession. Nicole found that amusing.

Athena sat a plate and silverware on the table. She seated herself. With a peculiar bow of the head, clasp of the hands, and a moment of silence, she then served food onto the plate.

"Thank you for the invitation. I missed lunch. Now, what would you like to know about Moab? I've lived here all my life, except for college and my mission, and I know the old stories. Moab history is fascinating and being lost. I've been to the museum in town and they don't tell the half of it." She commenced eating as she looked at Nicole expectantly.

"Well, history and tradition do factor in," Nicole frowned in thought, "I suppose." Honestly, she hadn't considered it, but now she was interested.

"Sure, it does. You don't want to buy a property if it floods every forty years." Athena poured a glass of water.

Nicole marveled at the girl's gracefulness. How had she become so refined in such a common place? Perhaps it came naturally to her. Although the fact they had been speaking in French made her doubt it.

"I see your point. Today, I looked at each house around town that might have suited me. Some were nice, but none satisfied my needs. This house may work for when we are in town, but the area is filled with beauty and I want to experience it. I need a property where I can build a home that will inspire."

Nicole stopped short of mentioning her mother and her need to convalesce. She avoided the topic because she didn't know Athena. Most likely, she wouldn't ever know her well enough to trust her.

"I understand that your mother needs somewhere quiet to recover." Athena laid down her fork. "Hmmm, I suggest you tour the parks until you find something that inspires you. You can't buy inside a park, but views from outside are nearly as good. If red rocks don't suit you, then the mountains are stunning and offer a vista of the canyons." She returned to her meal.

"Perhaps I did jump into the business end of things a bit too soon. I should have explored the area. How many parks are there?" Nicole didn't marvel at the fact Athena had already heard about Mother because the servants must have been talking.

"There are nearly a dozen State and National Parks near Moab. Would you like a guide?" The offer of assistance came with a friendly smile.

"Yes, I would, thank you." The sheer number of parks astounded Nicole and the prospect of a diversion delighted her.

"I have the day after tomorrow off. I'd be happy to show you around." Athena wiped her mouth with a cloth napkin and laid it on the table.

The offer to use personal time astonished Nicole. No such offer had ever been made to her by a servant before. "Surely, I can pay you to acquaint me with the area, though I'm moved by the offer, Athena."

"All right, we can go tomorrow, but I'd like to invite you to raft down Cataract Canyon with me and my singles group on my day off."

"Well..." Everything Athena said shook Nicole up. "I've never been rafting before." She pictured a drunken party of people nearly dying. She'd read a river-running article about that. "I'm not a partier."

"Party? Well, it is a lot of fun, but you don't have to worry about alcohol because the singles are mostly members of the Church of Jesus Christ. I guess you know we don't drink. We've learned how to have fun without drinking." Athena laughed. "I know you'll have a good time and you'll be safe, barring a catastrophic accident. The Colorado River is never something to be taken for granted."

The name-dropping of famous places and the promise of adventure won Nicole over. "I'd love to go."

Chapter Fifteen

Hangers clacked and squeaked as Nicole searched her closet for hiking clothes. She had nothing, not even suitable shoes. Furthermore, everything was black.

Memories of her father brought a tightness to her chest and a tremble to her hands. She remembered the tilt of his head as he had lifted it to look at her when he worked at his desk. His eyes always sparkled when she strode into his study with news of her day.

Even now she could almost smell his aftershave lotion mingled with freshly sharpened pencils. He had preferred Redwood number two. He always had yellow legal pads laid neatly on his desktop.

Nicole sighed, letting her hand slide along the sleeve of an unsuitable blouse. Outside the open balcony doors, she heard Athena's car pull up. No more time. She selected a favorite combination and dressed in the bathroom, surveying the full effect with satisfaction.

It was inappropriate for hiking in all the best ways. With a smirk, she sway-walked her high heels downstairs. Athena's expression of dismay upon seeing the ensemble was priceless.

"Good morning." Nicole strode past the servant in the entryway and proceeded to the SUV.

Bertrand opened the door for her and closed it when she was seated. Athena went around to sit beside her in the back seat. Bertrand drove them through town. They crossed the Colorado River then pulled off near the entrance to Arches National Park.

"Do you see that?" Athena pointed at the rock formation in the tight canyon.

Nicole squinted. "What?"

"This is a subduction zone. One tectonic plate is being pushed under another. It's rare to see this above the ocean floor." Athena beamed at Nicole.

"The highway is built right in the middle of it." Nicole frowned. "Do you think that's safe?"

Athena shrugged. "It is until it isn't."

Bertrand paid for admission to the park and drove past the visitor's center to switchback up the steep road. From there on wondrous sights unfolded. Athena called off famous names, like the Three Nuns, Balanced Rock, Delicate Arch, and the Fiery Furnace. Nicole enjoyed matching the sights with what she'd read online.

"I was in here last week and made some discoveries I think will one day lead to a landmark archeological find." Athena pointed at the vast desert landscape.

"Archeology?" Nicole hadn't realized Athena had an interest.

"I'm an archeology major at Southern Utah University. I've loved archeology all my life, and this is the perfect place to explore." Athena relaxed in the seat to gaze out the window.

Normally Nicole would have scoffed at such a career choice. But she had to admit, Arches National Park had her in awe. She thought she'd seen beautiful places before, but this left her speechless.

Athena knew all the stories and history. She talked about each place they passed. It was fascinating. Nicole enjoyed pulling over often for short hikes. She took hundreds of pictures.

The day passed quickly. By nightfall, it was time to return to the house. She'd only explored parts of one park and there were many more to see.

While she downloaded the pictures onto her laptop, she prepared for bed. She was exhausted, yet more excited than she had been in a long time. It would be an early start in the morning for the river rafting trip and she needed to rest. Lying in bed, she scrolled through the pictures again before falling asleep.

NICOLE BORROWED CLOTHES from Athena for the river rafting trip through Cataract Canyon. She felt ridiculous in someone else's things. Under the shorts and long sleeve shirt, she wore her own bikini. After slathering her skin with sunblock, she ordered lunch and drinks from the kitchen staff.

Athena drove them to the launch site. Nicole stood on the mighty Colorado River's bank taking in the beauty and splendor of the red cliffs on both sides. She admired the powerful river's winding ways.

It smelled like no other place on earth. Near the river, she wandered among sagebrush, yellow grass, and dark orange wildflowers, along with myriad surprises. Athena explained how the Tamarisk trees invaded the habitat over the past few decades, adding that these non-native trees had been drinking the river dry. Tamarisk-eating beetles had been imported to kill the invaders. In time, the river banks should return to normal.

Athena stepped one foot into the raft and held out a hand. Nicole took that steady hand and found a seat on the boat. The sound of gravel scraping the raft's bottom and the splash of water as it pushed off both startled and invigorated her.

Athena passed her a small box. "I thought you'd like to take pictures. I'm glad you left your expensive camera at home."

"Thank you. What is it?"

"It's a disposable camera. It's waterproof but it isn't digital. You'll can have the film developed in Moab." She shrugged. "At least you'll have some pictures."

"I appreciate the gift. Grand-mere wouldn't believe I went rafting down the Colorado River without proof." Nicole laughed because her grandmother might not believe it anyway.

Nicole had been absorbed with study during the past few years and hadn't taken much time for fun. Her society friends were always inviting her to Cannes or Nice or London. She had seldom gone with them. Once, she went to the Alps, but she preferred cross-country skiing to hot-tub parties at the lodge and kamikaze flirt sessions on the slopes.

She found her current company more interesting. Several guys manned the oars. The rest of the party ran their hands in the water or stared at the scenery as they floated along the river.

The current did the work, but a guide navigated for them. The young woman had a dark tan and long platinum blonde hair. As the group engaged in conversation, it turned out the guide was a member of the Church of Jesus Christ as well.

Everyone became acquainted. Before long Nicole knew their names. There were three redheads in the group, two men, and Athena. There were several blonds and one Native American. Then there was Nicole who, with her dark eyes, hair, and olive skin, resembled none of them. Not one person said anything negative and several guys flirted with her over the course of the day.

She hadn't exercised her considerable flirting skills in a while, and it felt good to be back in the game. To their credit, these men seemed sincere and more reserved than most. She received the impression it wasn't a game to them. However, they had fun with it all the same.

What surprised Nicole the most was how much she enjoyed the trip.

Some of the politeness and consideration was probably special attention paid to a non-member of their church. Andrew had always been that way around her. She'd resented it coming from him. But from this group, she felt like it was a kindness and that acceptance was her choice.

Despite the tightness of her life jacket, she sighed. Leaning back, she enjoyed the scenery. The clear blue sky was stunning. The moment reminded her of—

Why couldn't she ever have a thought that didn't lead back to Andrew? She should have gotten over him by now, but the memories kept returning. They had been inseparable for much of their lives and a friendship like theirs didn't just end.

Except, it had ended.

Athena jostled Nicole when she too leaned back. "Do you see those petroglyphs?" She pointed at the canyon wall.

Nicole squinted. "Amazing." She took out the camera and snapped a few shots with the clunky, plastic model.

The two of them chatted about the petroglyphs, the area's history, and about how many people died each year on the river. They talked about anything that came into Athena's head. She had a story for each bend, cliff, and pull-out.

Athena must have run this part of the river a dozen times before, yet her appreciation for Colorado only seemed to have deepened. Her reverence at times seemed intimately connected to the land. It was almost spiritual.

Nicole wanted a connection like that. In fact, it was what she was looking for when it came to the property she planned to buy. She wanted her mother to reconnect with reality and come back to her.

Thoughts of Mother distracted Nicole from the sights, bringing tears to her eyes. Somehow, Athena seemed to understand and put her arm around Nicole's shoulders to give her a squeeze. Then, with an impish grin, she splashed her with river water.

The exchange sparked a water fight on the raft. Before it ended, everyone was soaked and laughing. The river's pace increased and attention returned to navigating a patch of rapids before they reached their destination. The trip ended too quickly for Nicole. It had provided a welcome distraction.

Damp and smelling like a fish, Nicole was more content than she had been in years. A bus took them back to where their cars were parked. She let Athena drive her home and drop her off.

"Thank you. The river was amazing. Let me know if your singles group is doing anything again soon because I'd like to go."

"We're taking a trip to the sand dunes next Saturday. I'm borrowing my dad's dune buggy. Will you come?" Athena asked from the compact car's driver's seat.

"I'd love to. Thanks again." Nicole headed up the walk with her things in her arms.

She marched into the house tanned and happy.

Bertrand noticed her entrance. He took a sniff in her direction. With one eyebrow raised, he resumed dusting the study.

Nicole laughed. She climbed the stairs two at a time to take a hot shower before a good night's rest. It had been a long time since she'd felt optimistic.

Chapter Sixteen

The next Saturday Nicole arose bright and early to prepare for a trip to the dunes. Athena didn't disappoint and pulled up outside the house in a Jeep with the buggy on a trailer behind. Before she could walk to the door, Nicole ran out and hopped in beside her.

"You ready for this?" Athena grinned.

"Don't I look ready?" She'd sent Bertrand to the local stores to buy clothes.

"You'll fit right in." Athena put the Jeep in gear.

Taking off, they headed out of the gated community. They traveled through Moab, passed the entrance to Arches, the subduction zone, an indoor/outdoor dinosaur museum, the airport, and the entrance to Canyonlands. Then they went a bit further.

Off the main highway, half a dozen vehicles had parked in the sand. A dozen singles had gathered for the activity. The men set up an instant canopy for shade, and the women opened camp chairs underneath. All the while, Athena stabilized and unhooked the dune buggy trailer.

"Do you want to drive?" Athena flashed a grin.

"Is that advisable?" Nicole had never done anything like that before.

"It is until it isn't."

Athena climbed onto the trailer. She sat in the seat, started the buggy, and backed it off. Positioning it for a clear shot, she faced it toward the dunes.

Nicole trotted over. "Are you sure about this?"

"Yep." Athena exited the driver's seat, handed Nicole a helmet, and jumped in the passenger side.

"Okay then." Nicole jumped in and fastened the five-point harness.

"The gas is touchy, so take it easy at first. We don't want to roll it." Athena rested her hands in her lap.

Sand flew as Nicole touched the pedal. Piloting the dune buggy was tricky, but it felt like flying. She enjoyed every minute of the drive. Grit covered and grinning, she brought the vehicle back to the group of singles.

Everyone wanted a turn.

Chatting with the others under the canopy, Nicole twisted the cap on a bottle of water. With a deep breath, she enjoyed the ebb of the adrenaline rush. A giant red ant crawled up the cooler beside her.

"Watch out for that dude. They bite." The handsome redheaded man from the river rafting trip smiled.

"I'm not from Mars, I've seen ants before."

He laughed. "If you pinch off the head, then they're edible. They taste like lemon."

"I'll pass, thanks." Boys were so dumb.

A Native American man chuckled. "He's not kidding. We learned it in Scouts."

"Boy Scouts?"

"Yep, we're both Eagles. I'm Tom, by the way." The redhead lifted the tab on a can of orange soda.

"Is that a Mormon thing?" Andrew had earned his Eagle Scout award, too.

"It used to be. Um, you know the Church of Jesus Christ isn't Mormon's church, right?" Tom took a sip of soda.

"The Church of Jesus Christ of Latter-day Saints, yes, I know."

"Did Athena tell you?" The other man leaned forward in his chair.

Most everyone else had gone out to slide down dunes on snow

sleds.

"No, I knew a member when I was growing up." She'd been expecting this type of interrogation.

"Cool. Back in France?" Tom sat the soda on the cooler.

"No, my father was Console General at the Consulate in L.A. My friend was the gardener's son. They came every Saturday to care for the lawn and trees at my home." She didn't want to say mansion, it just didn't feel appropriate.

"Good guy then, huh? What else did he tell you about the church?" The redhead's eyes were vivid blue.

"I don't know, I wasn't interested then. I actually hated your church." How would they take that revelation?

Both of them chuckled and relaxed in their chairs.

"Nice."

"How do you feel about it now?"

The reaction set her at ease. "I'm not sure."

"And the guy, whatever happened to him?" The redhead tried to sound casual.

"I'm not sure." She stood and started to walk away.

"Hold on. I'm sorry for being nosy. Please, stay in the shade. I'll go if you want." He followed her and clapped on his BYU ballcap.

Taking a deep breath, she faced him. "I'm the reason my friend was sent home from his mission."

Tom's jaw dropped. "Wow. How'd you do that?"

"I'd rather not say." Guilt had eaten at her for years.

"Oh, uh, okay." He shuffled his foot in the sand.

She shook her head. "No, not that. But I went to South Korea to see him and when I went back to L.A., he followed me."

"What happened then?"

"Nothing." And everything.

He scratched his head. "Why did he come after you, if he didn't do anything?"

"I don't know." Regret clouded her emotions.

"How can that be?" He stuffed his fists into his jean shorts' pockets.

"Well, I guess it has something to do with the way I set my father's guard dogs on him when he tried to tell me." She made direct, defiant, eye contact.

Tom belly laughed this time, doubled over, holding his middle. "Poor sap. He must have been in love with you something fierce."

"You think so?" She hadn't suspected that, especially because Andrew hadn't tried to contact her since.

"Oh, yeah. Okay, come back in the shade. We won't bother you with any more questions." He led her under the canopy and took a seat. "This is my buddy, Cliff."

Cliff extended a hand.

She shook it, remembering him from the rafting trip.

"I thought Andrew was mad at me for getting him sent home." She smoothed the front of her tacky tourist shirt after she sat down.

"If you didn't do anything inappropriate, then I think he came home to propose. How long had he been out?" Tom asked.

"Eighteen months." Six months short of the two-year plan.

"See, it was fine." Cliff nodded.

"I thought men served for two years." Nicole frowned.

"True. But if you have a good reason, then you can go home after a year. It's still considered an honorable mission."

"Oh, I didn't know." Nicole had a lot to think about.

Had Andrew been there to propose? She found it hard to breathe. Maybe he hadn't been as angry with her as she thought he was. Although, after the dog incident, he should have been furious.

"Did you ever see him again?" Cliff avoided her gaze by looking at the sand at his left.

"No." She focused on oxygen.

"No letters, nothing?" A crease formed in Tom's brow.

"A Christmas package mailed from South Korea showed up in

February. It was postmarked in early December."

"Slow boat. Thrifty." Cliff smiled. "Anything good?" He had a nice smile.

"Um, not really, just Korean knickknacks...some gum."

"No note?" Tom looked a little guilty for asking.

"Yeah, about how much he loved his mission and all the people he'd met." It had been hard to read.

"I bet that twisted the knife." Tom shook his head.

She met his gaze, suddenly unable to say much, and nodded.

"Sorry." Tom pulled the ballcap lower over his eyes.

"Thanks for explaining things to me. I've felt guilty about it for a long time." She didn't look directly at him.

"Anytime. You know, you should come and see what the Church of Jesus Christ is all about. Sounds like you need a few answers to stuff you've been wondering. Will you come tomorrow morning with Athena? It's at eleven a.m."

Nicole exhaled. "Sure." What could it hurt?

Chapter Seventeen

The instant Nicole and Athena entered the redbrick church building, a pair of young men with black name badges lengthened their strides in Nicole's direction.

"Hi, we're missionaries for the Church of Jesus Christ of Latter-day Saints. My name's Elder Bello. It means handsome in Nigerian." The missionary's accent was thick.

She shook his enthusiastic hand. "I'm Nicole Moreau." He was indeed good looking, as his name suggested.

"I'm Elder Hardy from Sacramento. We hear you lived in L.A. It's nice to meet you." He extended a hand.

She shook it too. "I see my reputation has preceded me." Small town gossip had probably ensured that.

"Tom said we should answer your questions." Elder Hardy beamed.

"I can't think of any at the moment." Nicole suddenly wanted to kick Tom.

Athena laughed under her breath. "Okay, we're going to find a seat for Sacrament. Why don't you Elders sit nearby, just in case you're needed?"

Both of them nodded and followed closely behind.

Athena's struggle not to laugh caused Nicole to giggle.

"I used to be like that." Athena snorted with suppressed laughter as they entered a large room with pews and a piano and an organ at the front.

"This is the building' chapel. We receive the ordinance of the Sacrament here and listen to members who have been assigned by the bishop to give talks. I hope you like to sing because we'll be singing several hymns. The books are right here." She sat in a cushioned pew toward the front and pointed to two green books tucked into the wooden back of the pew in front of them. "The hymn numbers are up there." She pointed to the front where some numbered cards were slid into a wooden display on the wall.

Nicole sat down as an older man stood up to the pulpit to welcome everyone. The meeting proceeded with a hymn and a prayer. Then announcements were read and another hymn sung by the congregation. The sacramental prayer was said for the bread which was passed to everyone by boys in white shirts and ties. Then the same thing happened for the water. No wine, of course.

The prayers were beautiful. Nicole did not take the bread and water. If there was a God, then she didn't want to offend him. These people were so clean and honest looking. She was sure their past didn't include a sordid one-night stand with an assassin.

When the Sacrament meeting ended, Relief Society started. Nicole sat beside Athena in a room where the chairs had been set up in a circle. This meeting was for women only.

"You could have warned me that the church meetings were two hours long," Nicole whispered to Athena after the closing prayer.

Athena smiled. "I guess I should have, but I thought you knew. You seem to know some things and not others. What did you think of church?"

The two of them walked out the Relief Society room exit toward Athena's car before the missionaries had a chance to find them again.

"It's not what I expected." Nicole considered her answer. "I say that, but it is...somehow."

"I'm glad you liked it."

Chapter Eighteen

Nicole did like church. The utter lack of judgment from the people and the way they taught the commandments of God had put her at ease. Someone must have given the missionaries her number because they started texting right after the meetings ended.

The next morning Nicole came down to breakfast and waited for Athena to arrive. Dressed in gray, the servant breezed into the house. Nicole called her to the large table in the dining room.

Much subdued by the tone Nicole had taken, Athena came.

"Yes, Mademoiselle?" Her head was bowed.

"How does one deal with missionaries texting all the time?" Nicole raised an eyebrow in irritation.

Athena perked up. "Feed them."

Nicole raised the other eyebrow. "I could tell them to quit."

Athena's head drooped again. "Yes, you could do that."

"Would they stop if I did?" Curiosity begged the question.

Athena looked up. "Yes, of course." A crease formed in her forehead.

"And if I have them to dinner, what will happen?" Did she want to encourage them?

"I suppose we would eat." Athena tilted her head a fraction of an inch to one side. "May I come?"

Nicole's mood lightened. "And you won't be disappointed by the kind of person I really am?"

Athena's eyebrows shot up. "You're human. Why would that surprise me?"

"Fine. Dinner is at seven." Nicole swiped open her phone and texted the missionaries.

Athena bowed and went about her work.

FRETTING OVER THE DECISION didn't improve Nicole's attitude about the missionaries. By five o'clock, she felt openly hostile. The whole thing was a mistake. Bertrand's needling all day hadn't helped.

Nicole knew Athena wasn't an idiot and guessed that was why she didn't say any more about it. Not that Nicole had seen much of her since the cook had appropriated her for the kitchen. A formal French dinner was an elaborate affair.

Nicole stepped from the shower, wrapped her hair in a towel, and put on a robe. She would dress in a formal gown for dinner. She owned several. By happenstance, Grand-mere had sent her with a selection.

After perusing the closet, she narrowed her choices to three, a gray sleeveless, a blue lowcut, and a black off the shoulder, full length with a slit up to mid-thigh. She did her hair and makeup. Having made up her mind, she put on the latter.

The doorbell rang, but Bertrand would answer it. She'd sculpted her look to appear effortless and classic. Why? To feel confident.

She descended the stairs at a deliberate pace. Three men watched from their seats in the receiving room, staring at her show of leg. The missionaries had brought Tom with them. At least they were all dressed in suits and ties, though no one had brought flowers for their hostess.

Bertrand escorted her into the dining room and seated her at the table's head. The men followed. Perhaps because of this beginning, no polite conversation took place.

The array of tableware alone was enough to silence the men. The first course arrived, was cleared, then the second, and so forth. Her guests followed her lead when it came to the elaborate display of flatware.

Nearly three hours into the meal, Athena came in for dessert. "Have you enjoyed dinner?" She took the empty place at the table, chose the correct fork, and cut a dainty bite of tart. "Oh, this is delicious. I saw how the cook made it and I'm impressed."

The men looked nervous.

"There hasn't been much conversation. I'm afraid the silverware did all the talking." Tom took an overly large bite of dessert.

Athena sipped from her water glass. "Then finish your meal and go."

The corner of Nicole's mouth quirked in amusement. The evening had gone exactly as planned. Yet, the contrition and disappointment on the missionaries' faces melted away her ire.

"That won't be necessary. When the table is clear, we may have the discussion." She conceded.

"Thank you." Elder Bello breathed a sigh of relief. "However, I regret to say, we're past our curfew. We must return to our apartment. May we meet with you tomorrow around noon?"

Nicole took a deep breath and let it out slowly. "I suppose I could arrange my schedule to allow it." In truth, she had nothing planned.

The elders beamed.

Chapter Nineteen

Nicole had intended to speak to the missionaries about Andrew. Keep it casual. That was the plan. However, she wasn't even sure there was a God. The missionaries picked up on that and discussed the nature of God.

"God is our Heavenly Father and he loves us." Elder Bello held a Holy Bible in one hand and the Book of Mormon in the other. "We know this because he has taught people from the beginning the same beautiful truth. We can trust our father."

Trust? "I trusted my father. He said there was no God."

Athena nodded in thought. "What caused him to believe that?"

Nicole had never considered this question. She searched her memories of things he had said throughout her life. Father was generous with the ones he loved, showing great kindness to Mother and her. He was intelligent and opinionated, yet seldom spoke of tender issues of the heart.

However, there had been one time when he had lifted a glass of scotch...or maybe more than one. She had passed by his study on her way out to play and noticed his melancholy mood. When she'd come into the room, he'd beckoned her over and pulled her into a hug.

He had told her of how his parents had died on that same day when he was her age. It was when he stopped believing in God. It was when he knew he was on his own...until he met Mother and she gave him a child. For him, Mother was as close to perfection as he was ever going to get.

"Grief." Nicole didn't go into detail.

"Loss of a loved one can cause us to question everything. More often it reaffirms the precious truths we hold dear. Many times, it is what the loved one taught us that we cling to as we remember them. We honor all the good we've received by living in a way the person would be pleased with. I lost my older brother when I was five. I know he is happy to see me now." Elder Hardy leaned forward.

"You believe he sees you now?" Nicole had a hard time with platitudes and anything fake. If this Elder wasn't sincere, she would have him thrown out of the house.

He wiped his eyes, but more tears flowed forth. "Yes. You see, it was my fault he died. I ran away at a family picnic to go swimming in a creek we were visiting. I was in too deep and drowned. The paramedics saved my life, but I was in a coma for a month. My brother, his name was Aaron, committed suicide while I was asleep. You see, Aaron was supposed to be watching me and he blamed himself. He was fourteen. No one blamed him, but it didn't matter.

"I understand how guilt can eat you up. At first, it's a choice. But after you choose not to fight it enough times, it becomes a habit. Then, I suppose, it takes on a will of its own. We can choose darkness or we can choose light. They are both very real. I choose light." Elder Hardy held her gaze.

Nicole's heart hardened. "I'm sorry for your loss." It was a sincere story, but in horrible taste considering.

Athena burst into tears and embraced Nicole. "Oh, my friend," she sobbed, "they don't know."

Shocked. Nicole searched the Elder's confused expressions. It was true.

"Of course." Athena tucked her hands into the pockets of her apron and stared A dam of emotion broke free inside Nicole and she hurried to excuse herself. Leaving the sunny sitting room, she ran to her bedroom and flung herself on her bed and wept into her pillow. Father really was gone.

AS UPSET AS NICOLE had been by what the elders had said, she found her heart burning with questions. As a few days passed, the feeling of urgency increased. She hadn't spoken to Athena, not even when the servant had apologized.

Bereft and lonely, Nicole decided she couldn't lose the only true friend she'd had since Andrew. So, she went downstairs and found Athena polishing furniture in the seldom-used sitting room.

"I...hope you understand my reticence." The sentence was as awkward as Nicole felt.

Athena met her gaze for a moment and nodded before returning to the task. Lemon-scented freshness filled the air. Nicole's sinuses protested.

"Can you put that down for a minute?" Nicole wanted to talk.

"Of course, Mademoiselle." Athena set down the dusting cloth and curtsied in a most uncharacteristically subdued manner.

Nicole sighed. "I'm sorry things went badly with the missionaries. I didn't make it easy on them. Perhaps, I should have spoken differently because I do have questions."

Athena perked up. "I shouldn't have pushed you into meeting with them so soon. I'm sorry."

"You don't have to keep apologizing. It wasn't something you could have controlled. I needed to grieve for my father because I hadn't done that yet. But now that I have, I need to know where he is and how I can be with him again. Do missionaries talk about things like that?" Tears threaten to fall.

Athena nodded. "That's exactly what they do. They teach about the plan of happiness."

Nicole found that thought reassuring. "Can I tell you something?"

Sharing feelings about her family was not something Nicole normally did except with Grand-mere.

Athena stared at her feet.

The gesture of contrition amused Nicole and lightened her mood. She had no intention of firing Athena. Thus, she shifted gears. Talking about boys with a friend was something she wasn't shy about.

"I was in love with a Mormon boy, once upon a time." Nicole watched to see if Athena had already heard the gossip from Tom or Cliff.

Complete surprise blossomed on Athena's face. "No way."

"Yes, it's true. He was my best friend growing up in California." Nicole shook her head, letting some of her regret show through. "I made a mess of it."

Athena put her arm around Nicole's shoulders for a quick squeeze. "What can I do?"

Nicole teared up. "Tell me why I wasn't good enough for him?"

"Not good enough?" Athena chuckled. "I guess if he was knuckle-headed enough to say that, then you are probably a great deal too good for him."

Nicole laughed through her tears. "No, he's perfect."

Athena scoffed. "Not likely. Everybody's human."

"He's good, Athena. I've never met anyone like him. I always felt warm inside when I was with him." The feeling radiated like sunlight in Nicole's chest just thinking about Andrew.

Athena smiled her signature Mona Lisa-like expression of knowing. "He had the Holy Ghost with him. That's the influence of the Spirit of God. It means he was a good boy, but you don't have to be near him to feel the Holy Spirit. You can have that all the time."

"How?" Nicole desperately wanted to know.

"I could tell you the simple answer. Keep the commandments and be baptized. But I imagine you need a wider foundation in the Gospel of Jesus Christ before you understand me. And, of course..." Athena grinned.

"That's what missionaries do." Nicole laughed. "Okay, but not today. I need to go out and have some fun. Would you like to see a movie?"

"Now, you're talking." Athena excitedly moved as if to head for her car but halted. "Um, in about a half an hour when I'm done with the furniture.

The two of them laughed.

"It's a deal." Nicole headed to the kitchen for a snack.

Chapter Twenty

From the comfortable SUV Nicole looked through a pamphlet about the latest property for sale. Bertrand drove her and Athena directly behind the agent's minivan. Five hundred acres seemed like a lot, but a ranch on a mesa was intriguing.

The mountains were beautiful and good for grazing cattle, but they didn't speak to her the way this magnificent locale did. She wanted something signature. It needed to be a unique place in the world for Mother to look outward and come alive again.

The trees along the way oppressed her as thoughts of her mother nagged at the back of her mind. She hadn't seen her in over two weeks. She'd looked at dozens of properties and referred a few to Grand-mere for an opinion, but in the end, had rejected them all.

Nicole didn't want to go back to Paris, but she needed her mother. How long had it been since she'd admitted that? She knew the answer and the pain of not being able to talk to Mother then and now.

She'd lost her virginity to a man she didn't know in a way she didn't remember. She'd taken the morning after pill and was tested for sexually transmitted diseases. She'd caused Andrew to come home from his mission and when he showed up at her gates, she'd set the dogs on him.

Why?

Because she didn't dare tell her mother, let alone Andrew, what she'd done. She regretted everything, especially now that she was looking into the Church of Jesus Christ of Latter-day Saints.

Meeting with the missionaries had been going well...up to a point.

She felt particularly shameful after all the torture she had put Andrew through over it. But what could be done? Was forgiveness even possible? Could a single bad choice, one catastrophic betrayal, be overcome? If so, then when would she feel reassurance?

Longing for absolution filled her as she looked out the window and the car in front slowed to make a left turn onto a dirt road. She noticed the real-estate sign. This must be it. Two miles down a winding road the terrain leveled and they approached a ten-foot-tall gate.

"What is the fence for?" She craned her neck to look up at the top of it through the SUV's tinted windows.

"Um, Elk?" Athena leaned over from the seat beside Nicole to look at the paperwork. "Doesn't it have an organic fruit orchard?"

Nicole glanced at the printout of the listing in her lap, but there wasn't a need, because that fact had caught her attention when she first read it. "Yes. So, the fence keeps out the elk?"

"And deer, I imagine." Athena glanced around. "Though, I doubt it does much to stop bears."

Nicole raised her eyebrows fractionally and turned away from her friend to look at the cedar trees. She spotted a lone squirrel. Squinting at the nearest boulder, she discovered a lizard. No bears. But between the boulder and the tree next to it, she noticed a cactus with a little pink blossom. A desert in the mountains; she found it fascinating.

"Athena, what's the elevation here?"

"High enough most people thought there was no way to grow things up here. But there's a lot of alfalfa on the mesa, for those who own the water rights. Don't let the real estate agent swindle you out of those." Athena raised an eyebrow. "It has been known to happen.

"Anyway, my grandpa had a small ranch near here before I was born. He summered his cattle on the side of the mountain. He still has some pastureland just outside of Moab. That's where I learned to ride.

Do you ride, Nicole?"

"Yes, but not with a western saddle. I don't think dressage is the same as bronco busting."

The corners of Athena's mouth turned up in that Mona Lisa smile of hers. The sparkle in her eyes let Nicole know she had a mischievous streak. Having a friend like this kept her on her toes.

Nicole enjoyed the friendship because of Athena's genuine goodness, loyalty, and trustworthiness. This return missionary was pretty much the opposite of the society friends who abandoned her upon news of her father's disgrace and the scandals that ensued. They had sold her pictures to the tabloids and agreed to interviews for their fifteen minutes of fame.

Athena, on the other hand, wore Grand-mere's uniform and served willingly, but without feeling or acting subserviently. She did her job and invested her friendship as well. Nicole never told her she would have been fired under most circumstances for not being willing to at least act as a servant should. Truth be told, Nicole admired her spirit and needed a friend. Finding Athena in her hour of need had been a Godsend.

"I guess I'll learn to ride western style. Perhaps, I may even learn some rope tricks." Nicole laughed at her own jest and hardly noticed the ranch house, barns, and pear orchard as they drove past them onto the mesa's flat grassland.

In the field, a rancher tossed hay bales right and left onto the bed of a pickup truck. A kid stacked them as fast as he could. No one drove the truck. She did a double-take.

"How heavy are hay bales?"

Athena looked out Nicole's window at the rancher. "Oh, wow. I've never seen anyone pitch two rows at a time before. Hmm, about eighty pounds a bale, I think." She reached over Nicole to touch the windowsill. "I'm impressed. He must be made of muscle. Who owns this ranch? I can't tell who he is, but the truck looks familiar."

Nicole raised her sunglasses on top of her head. She squinted, trying to make out some telling characteristics. Unfortunately, the realtor drove on ahead of them, and Bertrand drove right after him.

They traveled to the mesa's edge on an increasingly rocky dirt road and stopped. The air conditioner kept the SUV cool. She dreaded opening the door until she noticed they had parked on the edge of the world.

Without thinking, she opened the door and walked toward the precipice. The panorama took her breath away. Looking at the layers of canyons on the horizon spreading below as far as the eye could see was like a religious experience. It awed, exhilarated, and moved her until tears pricked her eyes. The earth curved beneath the wide blue sky and a lighter blue haze faded in the distance, reminding her of eternity.

A hawk cried as it rode a heat eddy from the valley below, appearing directly in front of her as it ascended. This was the signature spot she'd been looking for. She would build a house near the edge and from the second story, her mother could watch the heavens revolve around her.

Nicole started clicking pictures. Grand-mere had to love this place. How long would it take to have a suitable house built? Could it be done before winter? Did the roads become treacherous when it snowed? She panned around and zoomed in.

"That's Moab below us, isn't it? This is amazing."

Click.

"I've never been out to the edge." Athena giggled with nervous energy. "I had no idea it was this spectacular." She pulled out her small digital camera, asking Bertrand to take her picture as she hugged Nicole to her side for the photo.

Nicole had never been treated like this before and Bertrand's expression proved it. However, he seemed discreetly amused. She read that to mean he was pleased to see her behave like a normal person.

She'd never been normal and never wanted to be. But everything was changing. Small d democracy suddenly appealed to her. It felt refreshing and liberating, French even.

Being on equal footing with ordinary people had always been frightening. Andrew had been her only common acquaintance. Why hadn't she given him a chance? Why had she been snobbish about accepting him for who he was and what he believed? Why had she never considered he might be right?

The answer became clear. She had given him all she had to give and it hadn't been enough. She hadn't been enough. She had never measured up in his eyes. That resentment was why she'd lost him.

It would have been better if he'd wanted her for her money, but he had never cared about power. He had believed she could be happier with what he had to offer than what her parents had given her. Andrew and his God saw her differently than she saw herself, and she hadn't been ready to change.

Mother and Father had persuaded her to believe he was wrong and they were right. She had listened to them instead of the voice inside her heart that said what he offered had value, not monetary, but personal. She hadn't listened.

Now, instead of a husband, she had Athena at her side. Friends were good, but she wanted more. Secretly, she had always wanted a house full of children, complete with noise, chaos, and laughter.

"Well, what do you think of the view?" The realtor wore a brown fedora pulled low over his eyes and a grin on his face.

"This is the property I want." She pulled out her smartphone and snapped a few more pictures. "I'm sending my grandmother the photos now. I'm sure she'll agree to negotiate an offer." Nicole finished sending the pictures with a brief message to be certain the water rights were secured in the contract.

She marveled at the pristine cellular service here in the mountains. "Where's the nearest cell tower?" She spoke almost to herself and then turned in a circle, searching as if she could see it. To her surprise, there it was, in the Manti-La Sal Mountains.

"Yes, that's it." The realtor pointed along her line of sight. "Excellent service up here. There are no wells, but the ranch has water year-round from runoff and it's clean. There is no natural gas on this ranch, but it has power and that's all that matters. When it's cold all one needs is a wood stove. Fires are cozy, and you could build an amazing home up here. I'm sure you'll be happy."

Nicole toned down her enthusiasm and nodded at the overjoyed realtor. He seemed a little too happy about the prospect of selling a multi-million-dollar property. He stood to make a large commission. With a sigh, she returned her gaze to the edge and walked as close to the sheer cliff as her pounding heart would permit.

Amazing.

Nicole's phone buzzed in her pocket. She let the camera dangle on its strap around her neck and pulled the phone from her trim black slacks. She scanned Grand-mere's text.

The older woman approved of the property and suggested Nicole retain the rancher as the property manager. She recommended up to forty thousand dollars annually for his work maintaining the property, including the orchards and eighty acres of alfalfa. The proceeds of which would go to the owner. Though, he could retain personal use of the ranch house, grazing rights for up to one hundred and fifty of his cattle and a dozen or fewer horses.

The detailed message stunned Nicole. How did Grand-mere know all this? Had she intended for her to buy this property all along?

"The funds have been authorized. Have you received the proposal?" Nicole's voice was deadpan as her mind wrapped around the text from her grandmother.

"Yes," responded the realtor. "I'll submit the offer. My wife can run it over to the seller." The realtor's smile broadened as he sent the text message.

Nicole took a deep breath of dry air and looked over the mesa's edge. Yes, this was the place. Her mother would love it. Nicole informed her grandmother by text that she had placed the bid, asking if she should move forward with preliminary plans for construction. Grand-mere confirmed.

Why was the elderly woman awake at this hour? The sun slid high above Nicole's head toward four in the afternoon, but in Paris, it was seven hours ahead and past the old lady's bedtime. Perhaps, she felt just as excited as Nicole.

She shrugged and captured a few more images. The lighting had changed as sparse, stratus-level clouds blew in on the horizon, lending more contrast to the vista. The wind would likely always be strong here on the mesa's edge and the weather changeable.

The sun's rays intensified on Nicole's face as if it would sear her skin. She decided she understood funny-hat-town, as she referred to Moab, after all. She would wear nearly any hat at this point. Alas, she had neglected to bring one.

Her throat grew dry. She returned to the vehicle for shade and bottled water. It was lucky Athena had remembered water and food because the habit of carrying it everywhere had not yet been engrained in Nicole. Before she entered the vehicle, she made a decision and called the realtor over.

"I need to negotiate with the rancher to retain him as a property manager. Would you be kind enough to take my associates back to the house in town?"

"Well..." The phone in the man's hand vibrated and he glanced down. "The offer has been accepted." He grinned. "It's fine to negotiate now. I'd be happy to drive them back to town." He loaded Athena and Bertrand into his vehicle and headed back the way they'd come.

Nicole strapped into the SUV's driver's seat. Though her US driving privileges had expired a couple of years back, she took the risk since Grand-mere had requested the rancher stay on. He knew the land and already worked it diligently. It made sense to keep him. She wished she'd thought of it herself.

Navigating the dirt road's rocky terrain, she contemplated what it would take to pave a lane to the house she planned to build. Perhaps, a gravel road would be best for all the construction equipment. Afterward, they could pave a nice road that would double as a landing strip for small aircraft. There were so many possibilities.

She pulled over on the dirt road's grassy shoulder beside the field the rancher still worked. He'd cleared nearly all the bales by this point, working fast. She picked up a bottle of water and twisted off the cap as she watched him. The realtor's vehicle continued traveling ahead of her, past the orchard and house on the way off of the mesa, to head down the mountain to town.

Bertrand hadn't complained at her sending him on ahead, but she knew he disapproved of leaving her defenseless. He had always been overprotective. Nicole lifted her camera and zoomed in on the rancher. He was closer now.

He carried a gun on his hip.

Wow, it was good Bertrand hadn't seen that. Did she have anything to fear? As the rancher rotated to face her, she tilted the camera to take in his face. Her heart clenched.

"For mercy sake, Grand-mere." She could hardly breathe. The old lady loved to interfere. Nicole laughed out one angry breath. "She knew it was him."

Nicole pulled her smartphone from her pocket and sent a text to her grandmother. "I'll get you for this."

The reply came back immediately. "Who, me?"

A demure answer, but Nicole knew the woman's sense of humor and understood the mirth on the other end of that message. She tossed the phone onto the passenger seat.

Leaning her head on the steering wheel she did something she wasn't accustomed to doing, she prayed. "Oh, God...help me."

The rancher was Andrew Leavitt.

Chapter Twenty-One

Sweat soaked the band of Andrew's white straw cowboy hat. Beneath its shade, he bucked bale after bale of hay to his younger brother, Jake. Both of them wore long sleeve cotton shirts and jeans with scuffed up cowboy boots.

Andrew tossed the bales onto the truck where Jake stacked them as fast as he could. This was the last of the hay in this pasture and it had received just enough time to dry before he bailed it. This was fortunate because the forecast called for showers tonight. Andrew judged the time to be almost five o'clock and his stomach growled for dinner.

He bucked the last bale.

Jake slid into the truck through the driver's window and hit the brakes before they took out the fence. Long ago, Grandpa had shown them how to put the truck in low gear and run it along the rows. It allowed two men to do the work of three. The ranch was always shorthanded.

Andrew ran alongside, popped the door, and hopped in. Jake put the truck in gear, heading toward the ranch house. Andrew grabbed the water jug and took a drink before wiping his forehead with the handkerchief from his back pocket.

The black SUV he'd seen earlier sat parked at the fence, and the driver watched them from behind dark sunglasses. He ground his teeth and decided he'd speak to whoever it was.

"Take the hay down to Grams' so she can sell it. I'll see you in the morning."

"Do you know who it is?" Jake squinted toward the SUV.

Andrew sighed. "A potential buyer, I guess. I'd better see what they want." Andrew opened the door and stood on the running board before nodding to his brother and stepping off in the field as the boy drove on.

Jake was only fourteen.

Andrew didn't hurry as he closed the distance between himself and the SUV on the other side of the fence. The engine idled and he knew the driver enjoyed climate-controlled comfort. It was an expensive vehicle, too nice to be up here, too shiny for dirt roads.

He clenched his jaw. Money. He'd never had any and never wanted much. But having to give up the ranch for the want of it galled him.

Taxes kept going up and the water assessment was outrageous. He sighed. Whoever this was, he hoped they would buy the ranch so Grams didn't have to worry anymore.

She'd be a rich woman and live out her days in comfort instead of want. He doubted she'd make any changes. But at least she could afford all her prescriptions and buy ice-cream for the grandkids. She loved to do that.

Andrew unsnapped and snapped the leather strap that held the pistol in its holster until he noticed his fidgeting. Stuffing his hands in his pockets, he glanced upward at the sky. He hated giving up the ranch, but he had no other option.

"Oh, God, let Grams sell the ranch, please." His heart broke as he prayed.

As he approached the fence, the driver stepped her shiny black designer shoes out of the vehicle and stood. Andrew tripped on a rock as if it had been his jaw and dropped to his knees. Nicole dove between the barbed wire. To do what, come to his rescue?

Caught high and low, she cried out in pain. Numb with shock, he reached out to help her.

She'd torn her black slacks on the front of one thigh and had a bloody scratch on her side. Half upside-down her white blouse slid up her back for him to see the cut well. She struggled to right herself, but only became more tangled. With a shake of the head to clear his stupor, he extricated her from the barbed wire.

"Steady now." His hands trembled as he took her by the slender hips and eased her through the fence the way she'd come. He unhooked her slacks from a barb and guided her head safely between the wires. "There."

She knelt on the other side and swiped at a tear, looking at him from behind sunglasses. He couldn't see her eyes. He had missed them, black except in full sun when the warm brown hues revealed themselves.

His right hand rested on the second row of barbed wire, and he swallowed the dust in his dry throat. "What brings you here, Nicole?"

"I just bought this ranch." She looked away. "I didn't know it was yours." Another tear slid down her cheek.

He could see the tension in her temple throb with her pulse.

"Grand-mere suggested I negotiate to retain the rancher to manage the property. That's you?" She glanced his way.

"Yep." Talk like this didn't make him happy.

Her breathing was shallow. "The job pays forty thousand a year and you can graze up to one hundred and fifty cattle and a dozen horses. Proceeds from the orchard and eighty acres of alfalfa go to me."

He wanted to be angrier than he was. In truth, he was upset and shocked.

"Thank Madame Augustine for thinking of me."

His suspicion stirred. He remembered the stately old lady and liked her, always had. But what if she had done this on purpose?

He knew her sense of humor and how much she loved her granddaughter. What if she wanted Nicole and him to get together? He frowned and pursed his lips. Standing up, he brushed off his knees.

"I'm not for sale."

"Andrew..." Nicole's voice quavered.

He looked at her, reached over the fence, took her hand, and helped her up. Touching her dazzled his senses to an intolerable point and he let go of her hand as soon as possible. He needed to keep his wits about him. He'd forgotten she did this to him.

He hadn't seen her in years, yet she still had the ability to make him love her. Yes, love, not just want, not just need, but absolutely love more than this ranch or nearly anything except his family and the Gospel. Thoughts of the Gospel firmed his spine.

There was little danger of romance due to her hard feelings against the Church of Jesus Christ, so despite her grandmother's wishes, this wasn't going to work. His heart tugged. Sorrow renewed itself as he gazed at Nicole. He would never love another woman.

He glanced at her left hand. No ring.

"Please, stay on at the ranch. We plan to build a house near the mesa's edge. My mother needs a quiet place to convalesce." She swallowed and faced away, staring at the horizon. "My father is dead."

"I'm sorry for your loss." He reached across the fence and touched her shoulder.

She faced him in a jerky gesture. "Oh, these things happen." Her voice thickened with emotion. The grief on her face looked fresh.

He pulled her to him with the barbed wire between them and hugged her gently. "When did it happen?"

She reached her arms around him and despite the barbs held him close. Pathetic sobs shook her shoulders. "A few weeks ago."

He'd never seen her cry. As much as it hurt him to see her this way, his body thrilled to have her in his arms. He rubbed her back. His rough, calloused hand snagged on her silky blouse. He looked at his hand with a deepening frown. He wasn't good enough and pulled away.

"I'm sure you'll find someone else to run the ranch." He strode on his side of the fence toward the ranch house. "The offer is good.

Someone will take it." If she'd been anyone else, he would have taken it.

"What will you do?" Her voice came softly.

"I'll start packing." His voice came out gruff.

"You live here?"

He kept walking.

She ran alongside the fence to catch up. "Andrew, I never meant to take your home. Please, forgive me."

His insides tingled and turned soft as his vision blurred with tears. He stopped to look at her. Emotion choked him.

"I forgive you." He wanted to reach out to her, but memories of the attack dogs she'd sent after him changed his mind, so instead, he walked on. "I just wish you could forgive me."

Chapter Twenty-Two

Nicole stared at Andrew's back. What did he mean? She had nothing against him, not really. He said he forgave her, and it seemed he meant for everything, but how could he forgive her for ruining his life a second time?

He'd been sent home early from his mission because of her, Tom said that wasn't true, but she still believed it. She'd set her dogs on Andrew for jumping her gate when she refused to see him and it was a miracle he hadn't been hurt. Now, she had bought his home out from under him and taken his heritage.

The wind shifted.

She breathed in the scent of the alfalfa. Rejuvenating air filled her lungs and she shielded her eyes with her hand as she glanced at the sky. A smile eased over her face until she realized how happy this place made her. That caused her to frown. She had no right to take this from him.

She pulled her phone from her pocket and typed. "You should have told me it was him. We need to back out of the deal. He won't stay, and I can't be responsible for taking his home away from him. I hate this, Grand-mere." Frowning deeply, she glared at the phone and waited for a response.

The phone rang with an actual call. "Hello?"

"Make him stay." Grand-mere cut right to the chase.

Nicole swallowed the lump in her throat. "How?"

"You know how." The old woman hung up as the tender tone of her voice echoed in her granddaughter's ear.

Nicole walked the dusty road to the SUV. Grandmother had given her permission to love Andrew, to marry a Mormon. But it didn't change the complicated nature of her feelings for the man.

Of course, she loved him. But time apart had given her the wisdom to know that being in love with a man was different than building a life with someone completely different than one's self. It just couldn't work, or could it?

She reached the car, lifted the door's latch, and swung it open. Committing to pursue him didn't mean success, but it did mean opening herself up to hurt. Was she willing to do that again?

She had flirted with the Gospel of his church and been tempted to accept it, but she didn't want him to want her because of that. She didn't want him to influence her faith in any way. Either God was real and he loved her and could forgive her for her sins or he wasn't. She needed to know for herself.

She clenched her jaw and sat in the SUV. She pulled the door shut and rested her forehead on the hot steering wheel to pray. Peace and a sense of well-being settled on her. She sighed as the tension eased out of her shoulders. The memory of the hug Andrew had given her a moment ago warmed her blood and brought additional heat to her cheeks.

She put the SUV in gear, pressed the gas, and drove to the ranch house. She'd take this one step at a time and see where it led. The path felt right.

Chapter Twenty-Three

Andrew hustled around the ranch house's kitchen making dinner. He'd grabbed a Lemon Boy Tomato, a handful of green beans, and a cucumber from the garden behind the house before he came in. He fried a hamburger on the stove as he sliced vegetables. With that done, he started a saucepan to boil while he snapped green beans into it. He tossed the ends into a compost tub and set the table, grabbing ketchup and bread out of the fridge.

He kept the bread in the refrigerator to stop the mice from chewing it up. Field mice plagued the Mesa. He shook his head as he set the items on the table. Why would Nicole buy this ranch? It was the farthest place from Paris, France he could think of. What possessed her? Grief, that's what.

A tinge of guilt set his feet moving again. She'd never find anyone to take care of the place the way he did. For one thing, incentives to work hard weren't there. Sure, a paycheck motivated well, but it only ensured a minimal effort. A man needed to be invested in the land, a promise of return for a hard day's work. She'd have nothing but problems with whomever she hired.

He shook his head. That wasn't his problem. At least she would try to maintain the land. What did he care if the ranch fell into disrepair?

He flipped the hamburger and stirred the green beans as he looked out the window. In the distance, her SUV moved along the dirt road. He watched it with his stirring spoon stopped in mid-air.

The smell of burning hamburger intensified, but he ignored it as he followed her with his gaze. She rounded the yard's corner and parked. He'd been sure she'd keep driving.

Grease from the frying pan popped onto his hand. He winced and shut off the burner. He never took his eyes off of the black SUV.

She stepped out and strode to the wooden gate, pulled it open, and walked up the crumbled concrete walkway to the door. The kitchen had wrap-around storm-windows, so he'd been able to watch her continuously. He shut off the burner under the green beans and waited for the knock. He imagined her looking for the nonexistent doorbell.

"Come in." The windows were open, so he knew she heard him.

She stepped into the entryway, closed the door, and took the two strides to the dining area, gazing at the table set for one.

"I'm sorry to interrupt your dinner." She avoided looking at him.

"Have a seat. I'll set another plate." He expected her to refuse his rural hospitality.

"I'd be delighted." She glanced his way. "If it isn't too much trouble."

He narrowed his eyes in suspicion. "No trouble." He scraped his hamburger from the pan and placed it on a saucer before he set about making another one for her. "It'll be a minute."

"What will you do with all your cows?" She sat at the 1950s Formica table.

He marveled at her citified use of the word cows instead of cattle. Everything about her stood in contrast to his rural lifestyle and suddenly made him feel insecure. Silence settled in as he brooded over a solution.

"I'll sell them." A sinking feeling hit the pit of his stomach.

He stared at the raw hamburger in the pan as it sizzled and started to brown around the edges. He'd worked for almost three years to raise two dozen scraggly heifers into the healthy herd of cattle he owned today. If he sold, he'd lose half the value to taxes. Ranchers never caught a break.

"What will you do then?" She folded her hands on the table in front of her.

He looked at her for a while before answering. "Go to school," he faced the stove, "I guess." He had worked the ranch full-time for long enough that he wasn't sure he wanted to do anything else.

He flipped the burger in the frying pan and tossed a slice of cheddar on it, then he set a plate in front of her along with the side dishes. "I assume you still eat meat." He fetched their burgers from the stove.

She laughed. "Yes."

He set the plates on the table, accidentally clunking the saucer. Embarrassed at himself for staring at her, he glanced down and folded his arms.

"Do you mind if I pray?"

"I'd expect no less." She clasped her hands in front of her and bowed her head.

The shock caused his jaw to drop, but he clapped it closed and managed a short prayer over the food.

"Amen." She reached for the bread. "Do you have any mayonnaise?"

"Sure."

He retrieved it from the fridge and grabbed a mismatched butter knife from the silverware drawer. He sat down again and handed them to her. His gaze lingered on her eyes. With her sunglasses on top of her head, he could see them. Her fingers brushed his as she took the mayo, and a thrill ran through him.

He wanted her. Yes, her body, but more than anything else, he wanted her. He needed her to love him. If she had only kept driving, then he could have suffered in peace. He pulled his hand away and put his hamburger together.

He wasn't hungry anymore.

He couldn't help but follow her every move. She assembled her burger and then cut it into four pieces with the butter knife, causing tomato and cheese to ooze from the middle. She skewered a cucumber spear with her fork and removed it with her knife before cutting it into small pieces, eating one.

He stopped himself from watching her chew. This was ridiculous. He felt like a fool.

Nicole screamed and nearly choked as a mouse ran through the middle of the kitchen on its way into the bathroom. Her knees slammed against the table's underside. He reflexively steadied it to keep the contents from flying onto the floor. Her eyes were wide and her face pale as she scanned for more before meeting his gaze.

"Was that a mouse?" Her voice was higher than normal.

He scowled at his plate. "Yep, I live in a house built on a field full of mice. There's no stopping them from coming in. You'll find out soon enough." He took a bite of his hamburger and struggled to swallow it.

She laughed. "I suppose so. Though, I won't be so complacent about it. I can build a better mousetrap given the right motivation. Trust me, I have the right motivation." Her mirthful expression faded. She glanced away before returning to her meal. Using a knife and fork, she took a bite of the hamburger. "This is delicious."

"I raised the beef. I'm glad you like it." His mortification over the mouse didn't fade.

"I've never known the rancher who raised my dinner before. It feels nice. Connected. I like it." She took another bite.

The sentiment surprised him. Most rich people who came to Moab resented the ranchers even as they ate steaks in the fancy restaurants in town. He would have suspected duplicity, but her remarks had been casual and followed by happy eating, so he accepted them.

He bounced his knee under the table. His stomach wouldn't accept any more dinner. So, he forced himself to stare out the window as the wind moved the branches and the shade tree's leaves rustled in the yard.

A fly buzzed around his ears. He reached for the nearest fly swatter and killed it without thinking. Unfortunately, he realized what he'd done too late to avoid the uncouth action. Oh, well.

He allowed the peacefulness of this place to distract him from her. He had enjoyed many lazy evenings in the hammock in the corner of the yard. He'd watched the stars come out after many sunsets.

He glanced at Nicole. Having her here, actually here, not just her memory, fulfilled a thousand wishes. But it was sad too. She would not stay, or rather, he could not stay, not like this.

Chapter Twenty-Four

Nicole watched Andrew look out the window. She became aware of the yard's details in a way she hadn't taken the time to appreciate before. A stone fireplace, complete with a metal cooking surface and chimney, had been built in the yard with a Dutch oven pit beside it. Several picnic tables were arranged around it. She imagined large family gatherings up here on the ranch. It seemed a marvelous place to escape the city.

"How long has your family owned this property?"

He blinked and turned partway toward her, though he didn't look at her. "Four generations."

The answer surprised her. "I had no idea." Her guilt deepened.

"Times have changed. Taxes are too high. The water assessment keeps going up. If you didn't buy this place, then Uncle Sam was going to take it one way or another. It's been up for sale for over two years."

"Have you had no other offers?" Her money protected her from Uncle Sam.

"Some, but they were all low. California developers have been circling. They want to build a bunch of cabins for tourists. They would keep the horses and a few cattle to give the dudes a ranch experience. They might farm the alfalfa. It's better that you bought it." He sighed. "I need to shower and go to bed. It's late." He shoved away from the table and stood. "I'll start cleaning out the house in the morning." He turned away. "You can keep the elk head if you want."

She glanced behind her toward the living room and the enormous elk head that had greeted her when she came in. She opened her mouth to speak, but shut it again and stood. Her chair scraped on the linoleum floor. She couldn't keep her hands still, so she clasped them in front of her.

Their eyes met.

"I don't want you to go, Andrew."

He cocked his head and noticed her torn slacks. She blushed but held her ground. His gaze lingered for a moment and then he walked over to a drawer under the kitchen counter, returning with a first aid kit.

He set it on the table, lifted the latch on the old-fashioned metal box, and produced a tube of antibiotic cream with fresh bandages. He ripped open an alcohol swab and knelt beside her. The touch of his fingers caused her skin to ache more than the sting of the alcohol. His tenderness had always melted her heart.

He smoothed antibiotic cream on the cut.

She had to grip the table's edge to silence her desire to tackle him to the floor and figure this whole thing out the old-fashioned way. She knew it wasn't something she could do, no matter how tempting the thought. Whether it was love now or not, she had always been attracted to Andrew. His newly filled in physique only made her desire more insistent. Although she liked muscles, muscles alone had never won her over before.

He lifted her blouse and cleaned the cut on her side, sending sensation up her spine and fluttering in her stomach. She breathed in deeply. Oh, yes, this man had powers she couldn't combat, but she would try. She had to try, in order not to make a fool of herself, not to mention compromising her principles, both the new ones and the old.

Thinking of compromised principles, she lowered her head in shame. She'd ruined her chances with Andrew years ago. That's why she set her dogs on him, and that's why she could never be with him. He didn't know what she had done. He would never forgive her if he did.

"What can I do to convince you to stay?" Her voice came out soft. She wasn't used to being subdued.

"Date me." He looked up at her from his knees in apparent sincerity.

She pulled away and faced him. "Why?"

He stared at a scuff mark on the floor.

Her expression grew severe with her lack of understanding as to why he would put them through a painful and senseless exercise when she knew nothing could come of it.

"You will never marry me." She'd revealed too much.

Blood pulsed in her flushed cheeks. She had dreamt of marrying him from the day she'd met him. They had only been twelve years old at the time. It was ridiculous. She was ridiculous. And it hurt.

It hurt more than she thought possible. He had rejected her. What made him think this time would be different?

"Why do you believe that?"

He stood up in front of her. So close. He looked down into her eyes.

She gazed at him with her wounded soul on her sleeve. "I slept with someone."

He took a step back as if she'd hit him.

She fled, out the door and along the sidewalk.

He caught her elbow mid-yard, turned her to face him, and held firm. "Was it love?"

She shoved him away, laughing with what must sound like a maniacal lilt. It had been the worst experience of her life. That was saying a lot, considering recent events, and the fact she didn't even remember it.

"No." She stumbled backward. "I got drunk on the airplane coming home from Seoul and woke up in a cheap motel with a man I'd never seen before. I don't remember anything about it except that I ruined my life." She paced in frustration, leaving out the further complication that the man had tried to assassinate her mother for some unfathomable reason.

"He wasn't the first, though, or the last." Andrew's anger clouded his expression, turning his eyes cobalt blue.

Her breath caught in her throat as a vision of the blood on the hotel sheet flashed in her mind. Andrew's thinking she wasn't a virgin had been deliberate on her part. All those years ago, she had wanted to make him jealous and dangled her suitors in front of him.

"How could it have been? I'm French, right?" She stepped further away.

His hands moved reflexively after her, but his feet stayed rooted to the yard. "You gave your virtue to a stranger?" Agony played across his face and his shoulders curled inward.

"It had no value to me if you didn't want it." On the verge of tears, she watched his response, ready to run.

He fell to his knees. "And there's never been anyone else?" He looked up at her. "That's why you set your dogs on me? Why wouldn't you just listen to me? I had something important to say." His head tilted forward until his chin rested on his chest.

"Whatever you had to say was too late. I offered you everything and had nothing left to give. That's why you should take this job. There can never be anything between us. We both made sure of that." She walked through the gate, climbed in the SUV, and drove away.

Chapter Twenty-Five

Andrew watched Nicole drive off. As the dust settled, he climbed to his feet and shook off his regret only to find in its place smoldering anger. She always had the last word when she should listen. If she thought he couldn't forgive her for one mistake, then she was wrong. He stalked across the yard to the hay barn, clapped on his motorcycle helmet, and kick-started his dirt bike.

He peeled out of the barn on his way after her. She needed to hear him out this time. Regardless of her answer, he needed to say how he felt. He had promised himself that if he ever saw her again, then he would tell her, no matter what.

He hadn't believed she had wanted to marry him. After all, she had asked him to live with her, not to marry her. Of course, that was probably part of the fashionable facade she had formulated to ensnare him as if he were a prize to be won. They had both played parts and their pride had forced their hands.

He wouldn't let it happen again.

Racing along the two-lane blacktop, he caught up with her parked at an overlook. He slid the bike to a halt, slammed down the kickstand, popped off his helmet, and strode to her door only to find her crying against the steering wheel. All the anger melted out of him. He breathed deeply, looking up at the sky.

How was he going to say this? He looked down at her. She hadn't noticed him yet, and given her tears, he didn't want to startle her.

Her dark hair shone in the sunlight through her driver's side window. He stood mesmerized by the rich brown hues. For years, he had wanted to touch that profoundly straight hair to see if it were as soft as it looked, or if it was stiff with hair products. The mystery of it was much like other things about her. He thought he knew the real Nicole, but did he?

Leaning forward, he blocked the sun from shining on her. She looked up at him. Her tears had run her makeup. He hated makeup.

"Take a walk with me."

She held his gaze for a long moment before she nodded in acceptance.

She had parked in a scenic spot, a recess in the mountain where a footbridge had been built to a trail made on the other side. It was mostly for rock climbers who enjoyed repelling off the cliffs. The sun was setting in the mouth of the gorge as orange hues lit the thickening clouds in a brilliant blue sky.

She wiped her tears with a tissue and exited the car. He held the door. Her expression remained subdued. To him, it spoke of her resignation to the status quo. He couldn't live with that.

"We can't leave things like this." He thrust his hands in the back pockets of his jeans to keep from taking her hand. "We've been friends for too long. Whatever you think of me, you have to know I love you."

Her bottom lip quivered. She shut the car door and walked to the railing at the edge of the gorge. He followed her, wondering what she would say. He'd never told her he loved her before.

"I'm not your sister, Andrew." She looked over the edge at the sheer rocks and resilient pines and cedars on the steep slopes.

He chuckled. What did she mean? "I know you're not my sister, Nicole." He slid in beside her, leaning on the railing to face her. "I have three of them. I know the difference."

"You love me like one, though, right? You want me to join your church. That's why you're my friend. It's a missionary opportunity. You have to love me because God told you to.

"I understand. It's just that I never treated you like that. I wanted you and I used some underhanded tactics to win you, but I never lied about how I felt." She held his gaze with passion, though her tone had been gentle.

Andrew's brow creased in thought. He searched his memories of their every encounter, looking for something to explain why she thought this. He had no idea.

"The Gospel is a big part of me, Nicole. I love it more than anything. I know I'm nothing without it, but I'm in love with you." He looked into her eyes. "You say you've always been honest, but actions speak louder than words, and I honestly thought you were just messing with me.

"You had many boyfriends. A lot of times when I tried to take you out on a date, you said you were busy. I thought maybe you liked me, but you seemed to be fighting it pretty hard. I'm sorry, I didn't see how you felt. I'm an idiot." He took her hand from the rusty metal railing and held her fingers.

"Why are you always calm?" She shook her head. "If I mattered to you, then wouldn't you feel some kind of urgency? Wouldn't you express some kind of passion? Wouldn't you cross some lines?" She glanced at him.

He took the opportunity to kiss her. Soft breath caressed his face and he deepened his lean into her. She raised her arms to pull him closer, running her fingers through the hair at the back of his neck.

He kept his left hand in his back pocket and gripped the railing with the other. It wasn't because he didn't want to hold her, but because, if he did, then he worried he would take it too far. He'd never kissed anyone but her.

The tip of her tongue parted his lips and he thought his body would explode with sensation. He pulled away breathless in a world floating with sparkles. Nearly deaf from the rushing of blood in his ears, he attempted to pull his hand from his pocket to steady himself as his knees buckled. Hooking his arm over the railing was the only thing that saved him from falling flat on the ground. Panting for breath, he nearly passed out.

"Andrew." She crouched to hold his arm. "What's the matter?"

"I need something to eat." He collapsed the rest of the way onto his rear end.

Of course, his blood sugar was low. He hadn't eaten his dinner. His vision spun, but he saw her run for the SUV.

Nicole returned with a bag of French chocolates and a bottle of ice-water. She placed a small round piece of chocolate into his mouth. He managed to chew and swallow it. She fed him another and another until he stilled her fingers. Gradually his vision cleared and his hearing improved.

She unscrewed the lid of the water bottle and raised it to his lips. He drank it, settled into a more comfortable position on the ground, and reached for another piece of chocolate.

"I'm sorry." His voice trembled.

She blinked at him. "What happened?"

He tried to laugh it off. "Don't you have that effect on all—"

She slapped him solidly. His head lolled backward and conked on the railing as he almost lost consciousness. She seemed to regret it immediately because she had his head in her hands feeling the lump on the back and trying to steady him fairly quickly. She patted his cheek until he opened his eyes.

"You're frightening me." The tremble in her voice made him believe her. He'd never seen her afraid before.

He struggled to regain his feet. "I'm fine. I just needed to eat my dinner, because I have hypoglycemia."

He held onto the railing with both hands and tried to regain his bearings. He could use some protein and rest. He hated his condition and had made sure no one ever saw him like this.

She stood up beside him. "When did this happen?"

"The doctor diagnosed me when I turned thirteen." He gripped the railing until the rusty metal bit into his palms.

"You never told me."

"It's embarrassing." He let go of the railing and waved his hands. "I never tell anyone about it, but I wear this, just in case." He pulled a medical alert medallion on a silver chain around his neck from beneath his shirt.

She took the medallion between two fingers and flipped it over to read the back before sliding it beneath his undergarment.

"Let me take you home."

The heat in his cheeks lessened as she dropped the subject. Passing out in front of Nicole Moreau had been a long-standing fear and now it had happened. Women didn't like weaklings. He followed her to the car and reclined in the passenger seat in silence on the way to the ranch house.

Chapter Twenty-Six

Nicole kept an eye on Andrew as she drove him home. There wasn't anything she could do about his motorcycle, though. She bit her lip because he still looked pale.

The sun had set, and she could only see him in the headlights of oncoming cars. Most people headed down the mountain instead of ascending it. She almost missed the turnoff. She managed to open the ranch's gates without his help. The car's rocking motion on the dirt road had put him to sleep. She wondered if that was all right or not.

Parking the SUV, she stepped out and walked around to open his door. He startled awake. With a grumpy expression, he undid the seatbelt and unfolded his great height from the vehicle.

He refused her hand and walked into the house. Heading to the kitchen, he slapped peanut butter on a piece of bread with a butter knife, folded the bread in half, and ate the sandwich in two bites. He slid past her in the entryway, went down the hall to the bedrooms, and collapsed on his bed.

She didn't know what she should do. Would he be all right? She couldn't bring herself to leave him. So, she sent a text message to Bertrand, saying she would stay at the ranch tonight. She proceeded to hunt for a room of her own, taking the one next to his.

Preparing for bed, she found a well-stocked cupboard in the bathroom containing supplies including a toothbrush still in the package. She opened it and brushed her teeth with his bamboo flavored toothpaste. The label was mostly in Korean, so she couldn't read it, but it had a picture of bamboo on it and that's how she knew what flavor it was.

How on earth did he find Korean toothpaste all the way out here? She shook her head and set down the tube. It didn't taste very good.

She unabashedly looked through the medicine cabinet. Nothing out of the ordinary and no condoms. She didn't have any either, so she wondered why she hoped he would. Her cheeks glowed with heat.

What made her think anything would happen? She wasn't about to let anything go on between them. However, she wished something would eventually change, because she had needs.

With a sigh, she grabbed a towel and a washcloth from the linen closet, she set them on the tub's edge. She tiptoed back to check on Andrew. He slept soundly with his boots on. She didn't dare take them off for fear of waking him because she suspected he needed the sleep.

The dresser in her room had clothes that could only belong to Andrew's younger brother Jake. She thought she had recognized him bringing in the hay with Andrew earlier today. She pulled out a T-shirt that even though it belonged to a teenage boy was far too big for her, and returned to the bathroom to shower.

Refreshed, she set about doing the dishes. Not sure she had put things away properly, but yawning from a long day, she headed to bed. Still worried about his wellbeing, she checked on Andrew one last time.

As she covered him with a thin blanket, she noticed the small stuffed monkey next to his pillow. She picked it up. It was the same one she'd bought for him when he'd taken her to the San Diego Zoo when they were sixteen.

He'd just earned his driver's license and had borrowed his dad's truck. When he dropped her home, they had parked in the driveway and talked for hours until he absolutely had to go to make curfew. She had kissed him.

It was her first kiss and probably his too. It was perfect; he was perfect, and chaste, and beautiful. She had tossed the monkey at him as she made a hasty retreat into the house. She'd been crazy in love afterward and it had caused their friendship to suffer. She regretted that, but not the kiss. She treasured the kiss.

Tucking the stuffed monkey in next to him, she went to bed in the other room. Nights on the mountain were cold and the bed smelled dusty, but she didn't mind. She fell asleep thinking of how it felt to kiss Andrew Leavitt and how she hoped it would happen again.

Chapter Twenty-Seven

Andrew awoke with the sun. He felt terrible and his head hurt. That probably meant dehydration.

He went to the kitchen, drank half a carton of milk from the fridge, and then entered the bathroom. Nicole's clothes hung from the shower curtain rod. In a hurry, he closed the door, wishing the lock wasn't broken.

He had to go, so he went, washed his hands, and brushed his teeth. She'd put a second toothbrush in the holder. His heart rate increased even further. She had stayed.

Why?

Guilt plagued him. What had he done? What did she expect him to do? Worse than that, what did he want to do?

He splashed his face with water and dried it on the hand towel. He ran his fingers through his hair while pacing the bathroom floor.

"I'll just make breakfast, that's all." He pulled the door open and there she stood wearing nothing but a T-shirt. He stared.

She gave a demure smile. "May I?" She indicated behind him.

"Uh, of course." He stepped past her into the kitchen.

She walked into the bathroom and shut the door.

He ran his hands through his short blond hair a few more times and resume pacing, this time in the kitchen. Just then a car pulled up outside. Andrew leaned over the table to take a better look through the trees.

Bertrand stepped out of a black car. He had someone with him. Andrew hurried outside to meet them.

"It's not what you think, Bertrand. I didn't touch her." Andrew came up short, halfway through the yard. "Athena?" Her pale face went pink. Great, now the whole town would know. "What are you doing here?"

"I took a summer job." The implication was clear.

Andrew wanted to slap his head, but he just clammed up instead. What must be going through Athena's mind? She was fresh off the mission and his Grams had already set him up on a date with her. She was nice, but just not for him.

Bertrand walked past him into the house. Athena stood inside the gate with her head down shuffling her feet. This was a nightmare.

Nicole came out fully dressed and in a huff. Whatever Bertrand told her had upset her. She strode right past him without a word, her head held high until she climbed in the car's back seat. Bertrand glared as he walked along behind her.

"Athena, drive the SUV back to the house in town, please." Bertrand's order caused Athena to frown, but she took the keys from his hand and obeyed.

Soon all that remained of them was the splash of puddles in the muddy dirt drive.

Chapter Twenty-Eight

Nicole sat in silence as Bertrand drove them down the mountain. The sting of his censure, 'this is not how it's done', didn't ease. Of all the people in her life, Bertrand had been the most constant. He meant as much to her as anyone. And for him to be ashamed of her, for surely that's what he was, pierced through every layer of her defenses.

She breathed through her nose, taking a deep breath to fight the tears. She would not let Bertrand see how much his words hurt. She hadn't done anything wrong, not this time.

She remembered how angry Bertrand had been when she'd ditched him in the airport after falling out with Andrew on the subway. When she finally made it home, he told her he'd been frantic and hired three private investigators to find her. She hadn't wanted to tell him about the drunken one-night stand with a stranger, but when Andrew showed up outside her gate, she didn't have a choice.

He had hugged her and made sure things turned out as well as could be expected. He had encouraged her to talk to Andrew, but she didn't have the lab results back from the doctor and couldn't face him, given the situation. In passing, she wondered what Andrew had wanted to tell her back then.

Bertrand glanced at her in the rearview mirror. Tension around his eyes spoke for him. She took one more deep breath and met his gaze.

"Nothing happened."

Bertrand focused on driving. The road twisted with steep drop-offs on the outer edge.

"Yes, it has," he said.

"No, seriously, we didn't do anything except kiss, once." She plucked at a piece of lint on her torn black slacks.

"You fell in love. Both of you did." Bertrand sighed. "I didn't know this was the plan. Madame Augustine is always two moves ahead. Why would she do this?"

"I don't know. It doesn't matter now, because I won't lose him again." She couldn't meet Bertrand's gaze.

"Will you join his church?" Bertrand's voice held disdain.

She met his pinched expression in the rear-view mirror. "If I join the Church of Jesus Christ of Latter-day Saints, it will be because I believe it and for no other reason." She cast her gaze out the window.

"Do you believe it?" His tone had softened.

"I don't know. Not yet."

Chapter Twenty-Nine

Andrew hurried about breakfast and his work on the ranch. He still felt weak from his low blood sugar episode, but that just meant he had to take it a little easier and be sure to eat. When Jake showed up in grandpa's old pickup, they loaded it with hay from the barn and the two of them drove to the overlook where he'd left his dirt bike last night.

Andrew rode the bike down the mountain with Jake following behind. Neither he nor Jake had a cellphone and Andrew wanted to find Nicole. He knew who he needed to call. He had to find out where Athena worked and thus where Nicole lived.

Andrew strode into Grams' house and found her in the usual spot on the sofa, eating lunch, and watching the noon news. Her frown lifted when she saw him and then fell back into place.

"The ranch sold."

He leaned down and kissed her head. "I know. Nicole Moreau bought it." He walked into the kitchen and made a sandwich.

"Isn't she the French girl from California?" Grams sounded surprised.

"Yes, and she asked me to stay on as a property manager. She'll even let me keep my cattle and horses." He poured a glass of milk and sat at the table to eat.

"And she plans to pay you?"

"Forty thousand a year. I can live at the ranch house, too." It was hard to swallow his sandwich past the lump in his throat, but after what happened yesterday, he forced it down.

Grams stood up from the sofa and slowly walked into the kitchen. "Are you going to take the offer?"

"I don't know. I always wanted to go back to school. But teaching doesn't pay forty thousand dollars a year, and I love it up there." He ducked his head. He couldn't bring himself to tell her he planned on making a complete fool of himself to try to marry a nonmember who hated the Church of Jesus Christ and probably always would.

"You have the money to go back to school if you like." Grams set to washing her plate and the two cups and a spoon in the sink.

"I know, Grams. Thanks."

She had promised to pay him for all his work these past years just as soon as the ranch sold. He knew she'd overdo it. Combining that money with his share of the family trust that held the land would amount to a small fortune.

It wouldn't be enough to buy much of a house in Moab or California, because the prices were inflated. But it would pay for a bachelor's degree at the school of his choice with money to spare. It wasn't enough, however, to impress Nicole. For the moment, he hardly had enough money to take her out to a nice meal.

"Thank you for tending the ranch. I prayed every day it would sell." Grams' voice grew thick with emotion.

"Me too, but..."

Grams patted his shoulder and headed toward the living room.

"Grams...?"

She looked at him.

"Where is Athena Westwood working this summer?"

Grams frowned. "In the gated community on Walker, taking care of some rich lady from..." Grams raised one eyebrow, "France."

"Thanks."

Grams nodded in her knowing way and sat down to watch the

news.

In a hurry, Andrew showered and dressed in his second-best outfit, semi-casual khaki slacks, and a blue, button-up shirt. He rode his dirt bike toward town and took a right at the four-way stop. Now he knew exactly where Nicole lived.

When he reached the property, the gate was closed.

Since he didn't feel much like climbing any more gates, he looked around at the cottonwoods near the creek and devised a plan. Gunning the bike, he drove off the road and into the creek bottom. Avoiding the water, he drove along the bank until he found a way in. He revved the motor and climbed the hill into the posh neighborhood.

Which house was Nicole's?

He parked the bike so as not to draw undue attention with its distinctive noise and surveyed the homes around him. When he spotted Athena's car, he knew he'd found it. He took off his helmet and mud-spattered jacket, draped them on his bike, and walked across the road to the house.

What should he say? The pit dropped out of his stomach. Should he have brought a gift?

He ran his hand through his hair to try to fix the helmet hair. He was what he was. It would have to be enough.

Nicole's words came to him about how she had offered him everything and it hadn't been enough. Remorse struck deep. Everything a person had to give should be sufficient. But sometimes it wasn't.

He broke out in a cold sweat as he knocked on the door. It opened. Bertrand stood there solemn and disapproving. A twitch in his facial muscles let Andrew comprehend the man's apprehension.

"I'd like to see Nicole."

Bertrand stepped aside and Andrew walked in. The house was big, but not really up to Moreau standards. Bertrand pointed in the direction of the study and stood his ground.

Andrew went in and sat in a chair before the great desk. A portrait of Madame Augustine hung on the wall behind the desk. Even from across the ocean, the woman commanded a presence in the room.

He received the impression he was here with her permission and under her watchful gaze. It was a little unnerving. Good thing she was on his side.

Would Nicole come down to see him? He chewed a fingernail as he waited.

Chapter Thirty

Nicole heard the dirt bike. Glancing out the glass balcony doors in her bedroom, she spotted Andrew walking up the street. Her heart felt funny in her chest, lighter. Despite the nervous flutter of her pulse, she was glad he hadn't let the gate stop him this time. She was also relieved there were no dogs for Bertrand to set on him.

A knock came at her bedroom door. She stood from the bed's edge and called, "Enter."

Bertrand opened the door but did not come in. "I've put him in the study."

"Very well."

A sliver of fear shot through her. Andrew may only have come on business. What if his grandmother had changed her mind? What if he had decided not to work the ranch?

She took a few shaky steps along the hall. Athena bustled about her work, offering a wink. Nicole felt encouraged.

Athena was for this, even though she had dated Andrew. Nearly every girl in town had dated him, per his grandmother's matchmaking network. However, none had gotten far.

According to Athena, it was mostly politeness and veneration to the pioneering family Andrew belonged to that made the dates happen in the first place. Especially since he'd come home early from his mission. Some women hadn't approved. Athena explained that it was okay.

It seemed the ladies of this town had all been on better dates. Nicole felt a pang of guilt, but couldn't help smiling to think of Andrew entertaining date after date with women he didn't care for. She hoped he hadn't picked them up on the dirt bike.

She descended the staircase and strode into the study, walking past Andrew. He stood when she entered the room. She sat at the grand desk with her Grand-mere's portrait above and behind her head. Sweat beaded on his temple.

"What brings you to my home, Andrew?"

"Oh, well, I wanted to see you." He worked the collar of his shirt with a finger.

"I hoped to see you again too."

She smiled at him briefly and sat still. The formal setting had her following protocol out of habit. It was defensive. Safe.

"Will you go out with me, Nicole?" He looked so hopeful.

"I'd love to." She stood and walked around the office desk on her way outside. "Let's take a walk."

Andrew followed. The clacking of her high heels on the sidewalk mingled with the rustling of leaves in the cottonwood trees. Tiny bits of fluff floated from the branches. The day bordered on ideal and wasn't as hot by the creek. So, they walked there and sat on a bench to watch the water swirl as it bubbled along its way.

She wanted to tell him so much, but this communion of spirit was their special thing. They had always had quiet afternoons in this park or that. He usually worked at some task his father had set as she watched from a shady spot on the grass.

One memory included a faded maroon ball cap from some feed store in Moab. How could she have forgotten he came here often? For two lonely weeks each summer he had been gone to visit his grandparents.

He had always returned with stories of catching fish in the ponds of their ranch, riding horses, and bringing in the hay. It was hay she now owned. He had no hat in his hand, but he was here on an unequal footing. She felt bad.

Glancing at him, she liked the way he filled in his khakis, long-legged and muscular. She had never suspected he had hypoglycemia. She'd looked it up online and determined to always have a snack in her purse just in case he ever needed one again.

She'd been frightened by his reaction yesterday. His grumpy attitude afterward had been unexpected as well. But the online information said it was par for the course.

He seemed to be lost in thought, watching something across the creek. She followed his line of sight, surprised to find a doe and a fawn in the shade of a thicket. The deer made their way along the edge of a field. She braced her hand on the bench, leaning forward to watch.

He laid his hand over hers, sending an exhilarating thrill through her whole body. She kept her eyes on the deer but she'd lost interest in them. He gathered her fingers, lifting her hand to take it in both of his. Warmth radiated from him, and she turned to see what his expression held in the way of clues.

He leaned in to brush her lips with his. The delicate sensation piqued her desire to do so much more. But she held back, afraid of letting her passions run away with her.

She did, however, return the kiss. The tenderness of it spoke of feelings he hadn't yet expressed. She hoped he would voice them. The kiss went on for some time as he held her hand and his breath whispered promises on her flushed skin.

Slowly, he ended it.

"May I take you to dinner Saturday night?"

"Yes." Her voice came out a little breathless.

"I'll make reservations for seven o'clock." He stood. "Grams' number is in the book under George Leavitt. Call if you need to cancel." His brow creased in the middle for an instant.

"I'll be ready, but it's only Wednesday. What are you doing

tomorrow?"

"Cutting hay."

"Can I see you?"

He smiled. "Sure. Call Grams' and talk to Jake. If you drive him up to the ranch in the old truck, then the Sheriff can have the day off from looking the other way." He chuckled.

"Why does the Sheriff have to look the other way when Jake drives?"

"Because he's only fourteen."

"Oh, well, fine then. So, I'll drive up, and you'll be out there on a tractor all day?"

They stood and walked toward the house.

"You can sit beside me on the tractor with the pull behind. You're lucky the swather broke because there's no room inside the cab for two." He took her hand. "Have you ever cut hay before?"

"No, but I need to learn." She gave him a squeeze.

"Well, most times, the only way things get done is if you do them yourself." He stopped at his bike and strapped the helmet on. He opened the visor and put on his jacket. "Have a good night, Nicole."

"I will." She wished she had kissed his cheek before he put on the helmet. Instead, she just smiled and shook her head. "Use the gate next time." Standing on tiptoe, she spoke the code toward his ear.

He smiled and rode off.

Chapter Thirty-One

Nicole met Jake in the morning and drove the old blue pickup truck along the mountain's twisted narrow roads to the ranch. What must those roads be like in the winter? she wondered. She parked in front of the ranch house and Jake hopped out to do his chores.

Today she had dressed the part with a pair of jeans. Who cared if they weren't designer. She wore a white t-shirt and a pair of hiking boots picked up at the local sporting goods store. She also wore a semi-nice-looking straw hat bought at the same place. Athena had helped her navigate the town and its limited supplies.

Online shopping looked like the only option for the future. But when she mentioned that idea to Athena, her friend became angry. Apparently, the locals had strong views about such matters. But where did they find anything if not online or out of town shopping?

Athena had an answer for that too. She suggested they check the thrift stores in town. Everything in the world eventually ran through them, she said. Nicole kept her mouth shut because she'd never in her life shopped at a thrift store. What would the society page in Paris make of it if they found out? She laughed under her breath when she realized she didn't care anymore.

She strapped on her other new purchase, a backpack with a built-in water pouch and a pocket for granola bars. Jake had handed her a handkerchief as well. For the dust, he'd said.

She spotted Andrew in a field already hard at work driving the tractor.

The pull-behind he had described grew more monstrous as she hiked closer. The whole process seemed terribly slow. The tractor moved so slow she easily caught up.

She marveled at the view from the sloping mesa.

Andrew finally spotted her and stopped the tractor. "Hello!" He spoke too loudly. He must be half deaf from the tractor's noise, not to mention the scything equipment it pulled.

"Hello."

It had never felt so awkward to say that word before. Part of her wished he spoke French because she knew she would be a little more comfortable with a Frenchman. Moab culture was proving to be a big adjustment, and part of her wished for things to be easier.

She took the hand he offered and climbed onto the tractor. He patted the fender. She sat precariously above the enormous wheel as he engaged the gears. The tractor jerked into a slow crawl. The scythe started cutting the alfalfa again.

Andrew shouted instructions over the noise and soon had her sitting in the driver's seat. Her eyes grew wide and her arms shook as she held the gigantic steering wheel steady. She did several passes but needed his help to turn the beast of a tractor at the row's end. Perhaps, one day, she would be strong enough to do it by herself.

She still wasn't sure she would ever need to drive a tractor and felt pretty sure she didn't want to except to be with him. His approving smile did a lot to keep her motivated, however. She drove until the alarm on her cell phone pierced the din with the unique alert she had programmed for lunch and snack times.

She'd asked Grams about Andrew's eating schedule and intended to keep him on it, despite the distraction she caused by showing up in his life again. Attempting to stop the tractor, she accidentally stalled the motor. Andrew pushed pedals and pulled levers until things were back in order.

"Why did you stop?" He leaned around her shoulder to look her in the face.

"It's lunchtime."

He flashed a grin and nodded. Reaching by her feet for a lunchbox, he backed off the tractor with his hand extended. Under a tree at the field's edge, they sat on the grass in the shade.

"I hope you like ham and cheese. I have lettuce and tomato to go on it. Here's a bottle of water." He handed it over.

She waved it away. "Drink it. I brought water with me inside this fantastic backpack I bought in town."

He chuckled and tossed back the entire water bottle in two attempts. "Thanks."

His sandwich soon disappeared. He looked through the lunchbox to find two oranges. He handed her one.

"I don't know how you work out here all day without more water than this." She pointed at the empty water bottle.

He was busy drinking the second and soon finished. "I drink a lot before I come out and even more when I go in." He shrugged. "I guess I'm like a weathered piece of rawhide. I know how to avoid the sun by keeping covered. I should have warned you to wear long sleeves." He pointed at her arms. "You're a little toasted."

Nicole looked at her arms. They did seem a little darker, but it might be nothing more than dust. She'd never been sunburned in her life.

"I'll be fine."

He laughed and stood up. He'd finished eating. "You're welcome to enjoy the shade for as long as you like, but Jake will be loaded with hay and ready to drive down soon. Will you drop the lunchbox at the ranch house? The door is unlocked."

"Sure."

"Oh, and don't forget to downshift into low gear on the steep inclines down the mountain so you don't burn off the brakes. There isn't much left of them." He spoke over his shoulder as he trotted off.

"Don't worry."

She stayed on the grass and relaxed as he started the tractor. She felt rattled to the bones and more tired than she'd been in a long time. Actual physical work was new to her, but to her delight, she enjoyed it.

She lay in the grass watching Andrew for a while. When the truck's horn sounded, she gathered up the lunchbox and jogged to the ranch house. Jake waited in the truck with a grin.

"I know, downshift into low gear on the inclines." She smiled back.

He tipped his hat.

Chapter Thirty-Two

Nicole showered when she reached the house in Moab. That's when the pain started. Her arms were on fire. It was a sunburn worthy of all sunburns.

Athena ran into town for some green gel to soothe the red, puffy skin. Aloe. Nicole had never appreciated it before.

She lay in bed feeling nauseated and exhausted. Athena teased her for not buying the hideous long-sleeved shirt she'd suggested yesterday. She pulled a bag from behind her back and presented it to Nicole. She must have bought it for her to wear tomorrow.

Dizzy, Nicole wondered if she should even try going to the mesa in the morning. But armed with her new shirt and a bottle of one hundred and ten proof sunblock, she planned to try. It made her smile to think of another day with Andrew.

When morning came Nicole drove Jake up the mountain in the old truck as planned. Her arms felt stiff beneath the new shirt because they were still puffy and sore. She popped two ibuprofen and drank a bottle of water, determined to push through the discomfort.

Things were just as they had been yesterday. Andrew was already out in the field driving the tractor with the pull-behind scything the alfalfa. She trotted over and hopped onto the tractor without making him stop.

He let her operate the tractor until he noticed her wincing as her hands burned in the sun. She had no work gloves like he did to cover them. He shut down the tractor because she still hadn't gotten the hang of doing that.

He carried the lunchbox as the two of them walked to the shade tree.

"It's too early for lunch." She didn't want him to quit early just for her.

"Nicole, please, I worried this would happen. Let me see." He reached out.

"Fine, but it looks worse today than it did yesterday." She unbuttoned her shirt at the wrists and rolled up the sleeves.

He winced and sucked in a breath at the sight of her angry skin. "I'm so sorry." He gingerly took one of her hands and kissed it.

Her heart rate elevated at his touch and her red skin throbbed with the increased blood flow.

"Well," she managed to say, though her voice sounded strangely low, "would you rub some of this aloe gel on me?" She used her free hand to try to unzip the pouch on her water-filled backpack.

"Of course." His severe expression of concern continued to scrunch his face.

He flipped the cap and squeezed the cold gel on her arm. It melted and slid off. He hastily caught it and rubbed it into the tender skin.

She winced. He slowed his ministrations, sliding his fingers under the rolled-up cuff of her shirt to reach the edge of the burn. He seemed to be playing by feel.

She patiently sought his gaze in order to convey her motivation for having him apply the aloe. She could have done it herself, but that would have lacked the element she desired. He did a double-take when he finally looked up from her arms. She rose to her knees and forced him to lie in the grass.

He didn't seem to know what to do with his hands, because he would just appear to decide and then alter course, causing his arms to flail. She paused above him long enough for him to realize she intended to kiss him. He stilled, his eyelids slid shut, and his hands rested in the grass. She lowered her body just enough to initiate a slow, sweet touching of souls.

She kissed his lips until he grew breathless. Then, she moved her attention to his cheek, his hairline, his ear. He chuckled. She laid her body lightly on his so she could move her lips down his neck.

She enjoyed every moment. Laying one last kiss on his Adam's apple, she lifted her head to look into his eyes. He stared at the sky, whispering something under his breath. She lifted her body above him.

"What are you doing?" Why wasn't he reciprocating?

His attention shifted to her with a start. "Oh, um," increased color blossomed on his tanned cheeks, "praying."

The answer surprised her, intrigued her, and for some reason delighted her.

"Why?" She teased.

He matched her smile with a grin and wriggled out from underneath her.

"A gentleman needs help to remain, uh, gentlemanly."

She laughed. "You sound like a character in a book. Do you still like to read?"

His blush deepened as he nodded. "I never got into watching television after my mission." He sat and pulled his knees up to rest his head, facing her direction.

She rolled onto her side in the grass a few feet from him, affecting her best southern drawl. "I have always relied on the kindness of strangers." She rolled onto her back and looked up through the tree's leaves.

"Hey, I've read that book and thousands of others." He laid in the grass with his knees still bent. "Books take me places I've never seen. But to tell the truth, it's the characters I like. I don't meet a lot of people here on South Mesa Ranch."

She tilted her head to look at him. "What types of characters?"

"As a kid, I liked Hobbits and Narnians. Now, I like a wider variety. I just want to know how people think."

"What genres do you read?"

"Everything. We have a great library in town. You should go see it."

"I would, but...." Her thoughts returned to the last time she'd driven into town.

She'd gone to buy clothes with Athena when a strange thing had happened. She'd been recognized by a large group of French tourists. The incident had forced her to make a quick escape as phones snapped pictures and people whispered her name.

"I'd better stick to ranching."

He smiled and rolled onto his side to face her. "You want to be a rancher?"

She wanted to admit that her true interest lay in marrying a cute rancher, but the words stuck in her throat.

"Yes."

"Then I'll teach you."

Chapter Thirty-Three

Nicole drove the truck up the mountain alone. It was Saturday morning and Jake had a youth service project at a widow's home, weeding her garden, mowing the lawn, and whatever else needed to be done. His level of enthusiasm for the task had surprised Nicole.

She had thought of American teenagers as being spoiled and sullen, having received the notion from watching television. Jake was nothing like that though. He was youth incarnate and seemed to love spending his summer vacation working.

She recognized the attraction of work because she'd always admired Andrew's work ethic. Though her world demeaned manual labor, she determined to openly approve of it from now on. She still believed in education and bettering one's self, but work should always be a part of a person's life. It was good for you. She imagined herself using a shovel to dig things and had to laugh. The idea took some getting used to.

Not in a hurry, she frequently stopped along the mountain road to take pictures. The scenic vistas and hidden treasures gave her a thrill. Each season must have its charms, and she couldn't wait to discover them all.

After a while, she noticed a Jeep stopped at the same places she did. The Jeep's occupant was an Asian man. He took a lot of pictures. Instead of taking in the best views, however, he aimed the lens at her more often than the scenery.

It gave her a creepy feeling. When he ducked into a restroom at the overlook, she made a break for it. Jumping in the truck, she drove up the mountain as fast as possible.

She drove along the dirt turnoff to the ranch as quickly as she dared. When she'd gone through the gate, she went back and not only closed it but chained and padlocked it as well. Always before, she'd done as she'd been instructed and just hooked a latch and left the chain dangling.

At the house, she found Andrew in the hay barn working on the tractor. The American phrase about having a roll in the hay came to mind. She couldn't help but smirk. She'd never force her gentleman to do it but could imagine how scandalized he'd be if she tried.

"Good morning, Nicole."

"Yes, it is."

His hands were covered in black grease and his knuckles were split and bloody on his right hand. He had the tractor torn apart and worked a stubborn bolt with a wrench. He strained, and she marveled at his muscles as they stretched taut the fabric of his black and white checkered shirt. Every time she looked at him, she lost her mind with wanting.

Taking a deep breath, she sat on a bale of hay, crossed her legs, and braced herself with her arms as she leaned backward. Rays of sun found their way to her face through the gaps in the boards of the barn walls. The wings of birds fluttered as they flew around the rafters. Fascinated, she watched them tussle with each other on the beams.

Something about it soothed her in a peaceful, healthy way. Yet, it was also invigorating. There was a rightness about her being here.

Even the drifting odor of nearby cows didn't bother her. Did Andrew still notice things like this? Surely, he'd seen it a million times before.

She glanced his direction to find him watching her with a steady, somehow approving gaze. She knew all of his expressions, but this one was her favorite. This time it was more intense.

"I got the bolt." He dropped the wrench into the toolbox with a clang and stood, wiping his hands with a rag.

"Is that good?" She shot him a teasing smile.

"Yes, but I need a part from the store if they have it. If not, then I'll have to order it. I need the tractor pretty soon to pull the baler so I can bring in the hay before it rains again. Can I ride into town with you later?"

"Of course, but you should drive." She glanced away feeling a little guilty. "I don't have an American permit."

"You don't?"

"No, not exactly. The decision to come was made in haste. I flew here on Grand-mere's leer jet. I'm not entirely sure she had all the paperwork in order." The words illegal alien came to mind and brought a bit of heat to her cheeks.

He put a finger to his lips, though he didn't touch them. "I won't tell." He laughed and waved for her to follow him as he headed from the barn. "I have a bunch of junk metal lying around that needs to be taken to the recycling place at the valley's south end. Will you drive me around to load it up?"

"I'd be happy to. But I must inform you there is no south end of the Moab Valley, not really. I checked to be sure, but the valley runs primarily east and west, not north and south. I don't understand why you and Athena insist on referring to one end as the north end and the other as the south end of the valley when that's clearly not the case." She had to hurry to keep up with his long stride.

He stopped at the truck's passenger side and scratched his head. "Well, I guess you're right, but if you say the south end of the valley, then everyone knows what you're talking about. If you said the east end of the valley, then no one would understand you." He climbed in and shut the door, rolling down the window.

"Moab culture is baffling." She ran around and climbed into the drivers' seat.

Putting the truck in gear, she drove around the property as he instructed her and even helped him lift the heavier pieces of rusty old metal into the truck's bed. Soon it heaped overfull. Andrew tied down the load to keep it from shifting.

"Thanks for your help today, Nicole."

"My pleasure."

They drove down the mountain chatting amicably. She kept her eyes open for the Jeep with the Asian man she'd seen on her way up, but she didn't spot him. A tiny knot of stress in her neck eased to think she had probably imagined someone following her.

Why would anyone pursue her to Moab, let alone an Asian man who looked like Dave Park? Her skin crawled. Then she remembered it was the Chinese her father had been accused of double-crossing and she redoubled her efforts to look for the Jeep.

Chapter Thirty-Four

Nicole sorted through the walk-in closet of her bedroom, looking for the right outfit to wear to dinner with Andrew. In a robe, she'd done her hair and makeup but needed something stunning. She hadn't brought anything truly impressive.

She knew Andrew would have frowned on designer clothes anyway, not that every dress she owned wasn't made by a famous designer. But ostentatiously expensive seemed to offend him. The flaunting of wealth offended Athena too.

Nicole sighed and selected her nicest dress, sapphire blue with heels that matched. She dressed and then found the right handbag, transferring the contents of her purse into it before heading down. As she descended the stairs, a knock came at the door. Andrew was punctual, it was six-thirty.

Bertrand opened the door.

Nicole walked right past him. "Thank you, Bertrand, don't wait up."

Bertrand's eyes narrowed. Andrew's jaw fell open a little as a blush colored his tanned cheeks. His gaze drifted to her plunging neckline.

"I'll have her back by ten-thirty." Andrew offered Nicole his arm and they walked to Grams' white Cadillac in front of the house.

Nicole allowed Andrew to open the front passenger door for her. He ran around to the driver's side. When had he found time to detail the vehicle? It smelled like jasmine. Andrew always surprised her.

"You look beautiful." He put the car in gear and drove out of the gated community.

"Thank you. I must say, you clean up well."

He looked good in a dark gray suit with a brilliant blue tie. The white cuffs of his shirt stuck out to make his tanned hands look even darker as they rested on the steering wheel. His knuckles were white from gripping too hard, all except for the ones he'd split yesterday working on the tractor.

She shifted her attention to observe the rural, desert townscape as it rolled past, noticing the area's poverty. People lived in anything they could find, it would seem, and everyone together. Nicer homes mixed in with run-down trailer homes. Even RV's looked lived in.

An immaculate yard would be next to one filled with junk cars and trash. She had studied the price of real-estate enough to know even the least expensive home on a postage stamp lot was beyond the reach of most of the people who lived and worked in town. The housing bubble had never burst here, the realtor had said. Without tourism, there would likely be no Moab.

"I've been wondering," she faced Andrew as they entered the highway that served as Main Street, "what keeps this town going, aside from tourism?"

"Historically, Moab is a mining town. The area thrived during the uranium boom in the nineteen fifties. Charles Steen was the man responsible for making Moab the Uranium capital of the world just when the country needed it most. We're going to dinner in his old house. They call it the Sunset Grill."

Andrew took a right turn off the main road. A steep drive switchbacked up the red sandstone valley's northern side to a parking lot behind a restaurant. It overlooked the valley, facing westward. He parked and ran around to open her door.

The back of the restaurant wasn't impressive. As they entered, however, the service proved excellent. The view of the valley from their table was breathtaking.

The two of them filled the time between courses with easy conversation. At around nine o'clock, the sun set. Over Baked Alaska, they enjoyed watching colorful wisps of clouds around the sun's bright orange halo.

"Thank you for this, Andrew." She felt more than a little moved by the extravagant gesture from this humble man.

The server cleared the plates, refilled the water glasses, and left the check. Andrew filled it out and slipped in a check card. The man took it and returned shortly with the card and the receipt. He nodded and left them to enjoy the rest of their evening.

Nicole hoped Andrew had left him a good tip because the service had been remarkable. She wished she wasn't worried about the cost burden of this date on the man she loved. He had no education. He lived in an overpriced and economically depressed town in the middle of nowhere.

The tension in her shoulders eased. It was the most beautiful piece of nowhere imaginable. She knew why he endured the hardships associated with such a place. As she looked at his rapt expression, she admired him for it.

He gazed out the window at the fading light on the horizon. Turning to look at her, his expression of contentment seemed to deepen. He took her hand.

She never felt quite as petite as when she compared herself to him. His masculinity heightened her femininity. His touch made her breath catch. It was the first time he'd touched her tonight.

"Will you walk with me?" He stood with her hand in his.

She arose. They walked onto a balcony at the cliff's sheer edge, overlooking the valley. They entered a grassy area with benches and watched the town's lights as the stars came out. High above the low-level light pollution, the heavens beamed with splendor. She liked the smell of the dry air as the cool of the evening descended with the sun's absence.

"I invited you here for a special reason. I've been holding on to this ever since I came home from South Korea." He pulled a white box from his suit pocket and went down on one knee. "Nicole Moreau, will you marry me?"

Shock stopped her breathing if not her heart. He still held her hand, thus keeping her grounded to him. Otherwise, she felt like she might have lifted into the heavens.

She hadn't expected this, not daring to hope for it, but she knew her answer.

"Yes."

He opened the small box and with trembling hands slid a modest diamond and gold ring onto her finger. He stood, taking her other hand as he met her gaze.

"I love you, Nicole." His voice caught.

"I loved you first, Andrew." She slid into his arms.

He held her tight. The familiar scent of his aftershave and the warmth of his body brought her peace. She'd done the right thing this time, if only she hadn't been so rash years ago.

Andrew tilted her chin with one finger and laid a tender kiss on her lips. His love eased her regrets, but the knot in her heart remained. He had forgiven her. Why couldn't she forgive herself? What would it take to feel absolution?

The word baptism came to mind like a promise.

She kissed him more fervently and slid her hands under his suit coat, seeking warmth and the contours of his muscular body. Surely, he was enough. Why did she need God or religion when she had him? Even as she thought it, she knew.

God was hers. The relationship was personal and independent of everything or anyone else. She wanted to feel clean.

Even more than she needed Andrew, she needed to be whole.

She wished she could share her news with her parents, but she knew her mother would not comprehend the words. It didn't matter, she had to tell her. She would send for her right away and have her here as soon as could be arranged.

Her father, if he were still alive, would have ridiculed the idea of marrying a poor man. He would have derided the idea of a need for a relationship with God. Marc Moreau had been an atheist. He had given his daughter money and believed that was all she needed for comfort and peace of mind even though his money hadn't comforted him in the end.

She eased the desperation of her kisses and leaned her head on Andrew's chest to catch her breath. What would he think if he knew of her new determination to accept the Gospel and be baptized as a member of the Church of Jesus Christ of Latter-day Saints? She hadn't told him anything about her recent introduction to the church, let alone the possibility she would be converted. He would think she'd done it for him. Since that couldn't be farther from the truth, she kept it to herself.

He held her in his arms as they looked over the town. The absence of big city lights had never looked so inviting to her before. She closed her eyes, feeling more at home here than she had in any other place her entire life.

Moab would always be magical.

Chapter Thirty-Five

Andrew's heart was full to bursting. He held Nicole and looked out at the lights of Moab with a permanent grin on his face. She had said yes. She wanted to marry him. What more could he need?

His smile dimmed and he pulled her closer. He wanted her to have the blessings of the Gospel of Jesus Christ. He needed their children to have those same blessings.

Nicole's parents had different beliefs and had somehow raised her without fighting, but they had left her without religion. Her father had won the argument it would seem. The possibility that such a thing could happen to their children chilled him despite the heat radiating from the red rocks of the cliff by which they stood.

"Nicole, will you come to breakfast at Grams' house in the morning so we can share our good news?"

"Yes." She snuggled closer as she watched the skyline.

"It will be early. I have church at nine o'clock." He rubbed her arms, for some reason she had goosebumps. "I'd like to take you with me, to meet friends of the family. Will you come?"

"Yes." She wouldn't look at him.

"Thank you." He held her for a moment longer, but the hour had grown late. "I'd better take you home. Bertrand will be worried."

She looked at him. "Come in, and let's tell him our news together."

Andrew smiled and laid a quick kiss on her lips.

"Gladly."

TO ANDREW'S RELIEF, Bertrand hadn't reacted badly, and breakfast had gone well with Grams. That just left the church meeting with Nicole. He drove them to the stake center for Sunday services.

"I probably should have told you that I teach the ten-year-old class in the primary. Primary is after the Sacrament meeting."

"You always wanted to be a teacher." She scooted next to him on the truck's bench seat, holding his arm and resting her head on his shoulder.

She looked more than a little sleepy. He couldn't blame her because he hadn't been able to sleep much either due to his excitement over their engagement.

"I called my family and they're very happy for us."

"Are you sure?" She looked a little worried or perhaps guilty.

He chuckled. "Yes, I'm sure. Have you told Madame Augustine?"

"She sends her congratulations. She will visit my mother today and give her the news. Mother is awake, although she's still quite ill." A shudder ran through her and she clutched his arm tighter.

"I'm sorry about your mother, Nicole. I hope she likes it here. When will you have the new house on the mesa finished?" He felt awful asking about anything pertaining to money.

He knew she didn't believe he wanted her fortune, but other people would think he did. What else could they think? He had nothing to offer. His shoulders slumped, causing her to look at him.

"Bertrand found a contractor who says he can build it within a year, but I want Mother here as soon as she is well enough to fly over."

Andrew nodded, understanding the need to have her mother close, especially now. "Which contractor?"

"Rasmussen."

"He's good. He'll be at church today. I'll introduce you."

Andrew pulled the truck into the crowded parking lot, parked, and

helped Nicole out the drivers' side door. She wore a conservative black
skirt and jacket with a white blouse, pearls, and black high heels. He
wished her skirt reached her knees, but he didn't say anything because
at least she wasn't wearing the blue dress from last night. It had been
dangerously low cut.

Friendly greetings, waves, and smiles commenced in the parking lot
and continued inside. Everyone seemed curious about Nicole. Andrew
introduced her and openly shared the news of their engagement.

Nicole shook hands with people in a more demure fashion than
was her custom. She stayed close to him as they made their way to the
chapel. They sat beside Grams in the pew she always chose.

News spread fast and soon people came to congratulate them in the
bustle before the meeting officially commenced. Andrew shook hands
and was clapped on the back until one elderly woman asked which
temple they would be married in. Grams' expression had never been
jovial but now it transformed into a definite scowl.

"We haven't discussed the particulars," Andrew spoke carefully.
"Perhaps you don't know that Nicole isn't a member of the church."

"Oh, well, I hope you two will be happy." The woman touched
Nicole's shoulder. "It's nice to meet you. I hope to get to know you
better."

"Thank you." Nicole's tone remained pleasant.

The woman walked to an adjacent pew and sat with her husband.

Andrew took Nicole's hand and held it until he felt the tension ease
from it.

The bishop stood to conduct and the meeting started. The
members' talks were pleasant and fitting for visitors to learn a bit about
the church. Nicole attempted to sing the hymns and even took the
sacramental bread and water.

He hadn't told her that those were a renewal of baptismal
covenants, but he didn't think it hurt for her to take it any more than it
hurt for little children to partake of the sacrament. In fact, he took it as

a good sign. It meant she didn't disagree with the words of the prayers to take upon her the name of Christ and always remember him and keep his commandments which he has given.

The woman next to Nicole noticed her receiving the sacrament. Andrew had seen the woman listening earlier, so he knew she understood Nicole wasn't a member of the church. Fortunately, however, she was a returned missionary and said nothing. There was no sin in taking the sacrament unless you had broken your baptismal covenant in a serious way and hadn't fully repented yet.

Andrew's mind wandered on with thoughts like that all through the meeting. He enjoyed sitting next to Nicole and had never dreamed she would ever come to church with him. A tiny hope warmed inside his chest and he sang the closing hymn with enthusiasm.

As the closing prayer ended and the congregation broke off for their classes, a few more church members came around to shake hands. Andrew led Nicole from the chapel, through the foyer, and along a hallway to the library. He needed to sign the log for his teaching materials.

"I should have told you more about my class." He gathered the supplies.

She followed him through another hall. "You keep saying that."

"It's a primary class with kids that turn ten this calendar year, then we have closing exercises."

"Exercises?"

"All of the classes get together in the Primary Room for singing practice, birthday songs, announcements, you know, that sort of thing. It doesn't take long."

He led Nicole to the classroom, glad to have her with him. Upon opening the door, he found half a dozen boys roughhousing as they set up the chairs. Two girls sat talking near the window.

His team teacher slipped into the room and shut the door as he took a seat. That was a relief. If he wasn't there, then the class would have to be combined with another one. Two-deep leadership was important.

Andrew wrote Ruth and Naomi on the board. He also secured a list of scripture references with magnets. That done, he sat behind a small table. One of the boys had set out a folding chair beside the table and Nicole sat in it, clutching her handbag.

Andrew squeezed her shoulder to reassure her. The snug classroom filled with six boys and two girls settled in as Andrew greeted them. He asked for volunteers to say the opening prayer. As three hands went up, Nicole's expression brightened with surprise. Andrew selected a stout brown-haired boy who offered a reverent prayer of his own quirky composition.

"Thank you, Trent. I want to introduce everyone to my fiancée, Nicole Moreau. We've known each other since we were twelve. She's my best friend." Andrew flipped open his Bible.

"You're going to get married!" A pretty little girl in a burgundy velvet dress stopped tapping the ankle of a boy next to her.

"Yes, Emma." Andrew beamed.

"Wow!"

"We never thought you'd get married."

"My sister is going to be sad."

"That's great!

"When?"

Nearly every child spoke at once.

"Okay." Andrew laughed. "We haven't talked about the details. Nicole isn't a member of the church, so this is our chance to make a good impression. I hope you'll make her feel welcome. Now, today's lesson is about Ruth and Naomi." Andrew started right into the lesson and the children followed along with him.

At one point in the lesson's middle, a new girl in a trendy skirt and cute top asked, "What church does she go to?"

"I'll let Nicole answer that."

Everyone's attention focused on Nicole.

She pulled a chain around her neck and raised the crucifix from inside her blouse.

"Well, my mother is Catholic. She wanted me to be Catholic too, but my father was an atheist, so I kind of grew up without religion. Now that I'm grown up, I still haven't decided what I believe. But I've been thinking about it a lot lately." Nicole tucked the crucifix back under her blouse.

Andrew hadn't realized she felt that way. It brought tears to his eyes. He hastily returned to teaching the lesson so she wouldn't see how much he hoped she chose the Church of Jesus Christ of Latter-day Saints.

He wanted it desperately, but he wouldn't push her. It wasn't a condition of his love as she had once believed. He still felt bad about her mistaken impression. But at least now, he understood her behavior years ago.

Chapter Thirty-Six

Nicole enjoyed the lesson Andrew taught and the enthusiastic, if somewhat rowdy, children in Andrew's class. She'd never heard about Ruth or the customs of the day. Boaz impressed her with how generous he was to the poor by leaving the corners of the fields for them to glean.

However, it was infuriating to think of Ruth having to bow at the end of his bed to obtain his willingness to fulfill his responsibilities as a husband. It surprised her that Ruth's humility and willingness to accept the Gospel, even though she was a foreigner, had gained her such an amazing promise from God. Her line brought forth the Savior of the world.

Nicole didn't know much about the Bible. But she knew there weren't many women mentioned in it, let alone books dedicated to them. It was an honor. It meant that God didn't hold back his blessings from people who weren't born into his church. Somehow, knowing that comforted her.

Sharing Time in the primary was far more fun than Nicole imagined church could be. The Primary Presidency astounded her. Outside the professional arena, she'd never seen such capable women.

They radiated incredible power.

They bore testimony with tenderness and authority. The children responded to their instructions in such positive ways. It was impressive to see how they managed the children's enthusiasm with patience and affection.

The exuberance of these children might, in any other setting, have been viewed as out of control or inappropriate. But it wasn't. Somehow, the fact they were managed and respectful in their way made it a safe, open environment for learning.

They sang wiggle songs and participated in activities. They learned new children's hymns. They earned rewards for participating by offering prayers, talks, themes, and scriptures. Everyone seemed to know how things were done, except Nicole, but she fit into the process comfortably.

The meetings dismissed with prayer and Nicole felt lighter in spirit, though physically exhausted. She hadn't slept last night. It seemed like a dream to be engaged to Andrew after all these years. She wanted to fast forward to when they could just be married people with all the decisions and trials standing between them resolved.

She had come to church today with some apprehension about being recognized. However, tucked away in the primary, she had avoided that, thankfully. She caught Andrew's arm, because she could, and walked beside him on their way out of the building. A short, wavy-haired man with bright blue eyes and a jovial smile came up and shook their hands with a firm, enthusiastic grip.

"May I speak with both of you for a minute?"

"Sure, Bishop." Andrew smiled.

Nicole nodded, but she didn't feel at ease with the prospect. What could the bishop have to talk to them about except morality? She sighed and followed along.

He led them into an office with a large desk and several cushioned folding chairs. She noticed the Savior's picture on the wall. It was the kindest version she'd ever seen and the man depicted in it had a spark of enthusiastic merriment in his eyes that reminded her of the children she'd observed today.

"I wanted to get to know you, Nicole. I'm Bishop Brad Jolly. I own and operate a parts store in town. I'm married with six children who are almost all grown. One of my daughters is on a mission in Africa, French-speaking. I hear you are from France." Bishop took a seat behind the desk.

Andrew and Nicole sat beside one another in front of the desk.

"Yes, I'm French. However, Andrew and I grew up together during my father's time at the consulate in Los Angeles." Nicole tried not to fidget with her handbag.

"I'm happy you two have found each other again. I see the depth of your love for one another. Congratulations on your engagement."

"Thank you," Nicole and Andrew said.

"Do you have plans for the wedding? It's come to my attention you're not a member of the church, Nicole. I hope you feel welcome here. If you choose to be married in this building or have a reception here, then I want you to feel at ease. If you need someone to perform the ceremony, then you need only ask. I would be happy to be of assistance." Bishop looked hopeful.

"We haven't discussed it," Nicole answered.

The question surprised her. She hadn't considered being married in Moab.

"I hope you won't wait too long. The world would teach us there is nothing wrong with being intimate before marriage, but the Lord has given us commandments that if followed lead to happiness." Bishop slid a pamphlet across the desk that read, For the Strength of Youth. "I hope you will read this and abide by the guidelines. No nudity and no touching intimate places even with clothing on before marriage. It is for our safety and happiness that the Lord counsels us to be patient. Trust me, the rewards are worth it."

Nicole felt her face flush with heat. She avoided looking at the bishop and didn't take the pamphlet. Andrew reached forward and took it.

Surely, he didn't need it. She was the one with the disgraceful past and the propensity toward inappropriate behavior. Had Andrew set this up? Had he told the bishop what she had done? She wanted to leave this place.

"Thank you, Bishop." Andrew took Nicole's hand and together they stood.

"Nicole, may I speak to you alone for a moment?" Bishop's voice was gentle and his eyes compassionate.

She nodded since she couldn't speak past the emotional response she'd had to his apparent censure.

"I'll be right outside." Andrew squeezed her hand, left the room, and shut the door.

"Did Andrew talk to you about me?"

"No."

The tension in her shoulders didn't ease much.

Bishop sat and looked at her until she met his gaze. He wasn't accusing her. His expression of patient kindness melted her anger by easing her fear.

"Part of a bishop's job is to listen."

The tone of his voice brought a warm feeling to her heart, causing her emotions to dissolve into tears.

"Is forgiveness really possible?"

"Yes." There was no equivocation in his tone.

"I need to be forgiven. Do you give absolution?"

"Forgiveness comes from God. It's my special calling to help God's children work out their repentance, so they can have all the blessings our Heavenly Father has to offer. Have you and Andrew done anything you shouldn't?"

"No, but I slept with a man a few years back. I can't forgive myself for it. Andrew forgives me, but I still feel like I betrayed him. I don't know what to do."

"Did you love this other man?" Bishop's question surprised her.

"No! He was a stranger. I had argued with Andrew, and to make it worse, I drank too much on a flight home from Korea. I drank even more in an airport bar. The man came up and offered to take me to dinner. I went with him, but I don't remember anything until I woke up in a cheap hotel.

"I shouldn't have gotten drunk. I hardly ever drink. I took the morning-after pill." She glanced at Bishop, but he didn't look upset.

"I know that was wrong, but the man didn't use protection, and I didn't know what else to do." She worried her fingers in her lap.

Bishop looked worried. "You were so drunk you blacked out, and the stranger from the bar didn't take you to dinner but instead took you to a hotel and took advantage of you?"

"Yes."

"Nicole, have you considered you may have been sexually assaulted?"

"No!" She met Bishop's eyes and saw they held no blame, only deep compassion.

It made her think. She had been bruised and in pain when she woke up. She had been too drunk to consent. She certainly wouldn't have consented if she'd been sober.

However, she had gone with Dave Park and it had happened. It was her fault because she had chosen to drink too much. What man wouldn't have taken advantage of the situation?

Andrew. He would never have hurt her.

"The stranger you met in the bar had absolute power over you because you were incapacitated by alcohol and grief over your fight with Andrew I imagine. Any decent man would have called you a cab and sent you home, but not that man. You blame yourself, but you need to consider your character and the choices you've made your whole life. Do you think you chose to sleep with that man or did he force himself on you?"

"I wasn't raped. I'm not a victim." Nicole stood and paced.

"You survived something you didn't choose. You need to forgive yourself for drinking too much and turn to the Lord for healing. God loves you, Nicole."

"If he loves me then why didn't he stop me? Why did he let it happen?" Resentment mingled with a lack of understanding.

"God doesn't make people's choices for them. There would be no point to this life if he did. You made a simple mistake, one that wasn't even against your beliefs. The man who assaulted you is the one who sinned."

"I took the morning after pill. That's against my beliefs."

"You prevented the possibility of a pregnancy you didn't want and hadn't consented to. It wasn't an abortion. It wasn't murder or anything like it. I don't know what religion you belong to, but I hope you will pray and read the scriptures. Seek out the Lord and find comfort, Nicole. I'm here to talk if you need to." Bishop didn't stand up. He seemed to be waiting for her to decide what she wanted to do.

"Thank you. I'd better go." She'd done more than enough talking for today.

A shiver of upset ran through her, but his words made sense and the warmth of them filled the room like a blanket of sunlight. She wanted to feel that sunlight inside her heart, but the icy knot of guilt she carried hadn't thawed completely. She walked over and grasped the door handle.

"I'll pray about it."

Chapter Thirty-Seven

A ndrew stood when Nicole came out of Bishop's office, but she simply walked past him on the way to the truck. Bishop looked sad and a little concerned, but Andrew didn't have time to ask why. Bishop wouldn't have told him anyway.

He followed Nicole through the hallway and out to the truck, unlocked it, and she slid in. He climbed in after her and started it, but before he put it in gear, he took a deep breath.

"Are you all right, Nicole?" He looked at his hands on the steering wheel. Whatever had gone wrong had upset her. She'd been crying and her cheeks were flushed.

"I don't want to talk about it."

"I'll take you home."

He drove from the parking lot. They were near her house before she slid over and linked arms with him. She rested her head on his shoulder and closed her eyes. He relaxed a little and enjoyed the closeness.

"Are you going to be all right?"

"I'm fine." She didn't open her eyes. "Will you dine at the house this evening?"

"I have to go up the mountain tonight so I can feed the animals and rotate the water in the morning."

"Then come over now. Come to lunch."

He found her hand and lifted it to his lips. "I'd be happy to."

The meal was quiet. Though the table was formal, Nicole had come

146

to his side of it and sat close to him. She touched his arm or his hand often as if needing comfort or reassurance, but she never talked about what she'd discussed with Bishop.

When it was time for him to go, she stood with him in the secluded entryway. She held his hands for a moment as if she wanted to say something. Instead, she simply hugged him.

He held her close and laid a kiss on her head. He wished she would kiss him. Something wasn't right. He held her closer.

"I love you, Nicole."

A shiver ran through her.

"I love you too, Andrew." She looked up at him.

He closed in for a kiss, but it wasn't the same as it had been. She broke it off quickly. A trickle of panic worked through him.

"When can I see you again?"

"I'm closing on the property in the morning. I'll drive to the ranch after I sign the papers. I'll bring a picnic lunch. I'd like to see the mountains. I've heard about how pretty the lakes are." She sounded stiff.

Andrew had an idea. "I'll take you to Oowah. Wear your swimsuit." He grinned.

She relaxed into a smile. "What are you up to, Andrew Leavitt?"

How did she always know when he planned mischief?

"It's a long-standing tradition. You wouldn't want to go against tradition, would you?"

"If you push me in, then I'll return the favor!"

"Oh, you will, will you?" He tickled her.

She wriggled away from him until he caught her again and kissed her properly this time. She seemed to enjoy his affection now. He had to pull back before he became too excited.

Holding onto his middle, she wouldn't let him loose and buried her face in his chest. He held her while he caught his breath. At last, she eased her embrace and allowed him to leave.

Chapter Thirty-Eight

Nicole placed a picnic basket in the passenger seat before driving the black SUV up the mountain. She wore her bikini under her clothes. She wore short shorts and a long-sleeve white shirt open and tied at the waist. Additionally, she wore her customary sunglasses, a sunhat, and sandals. She brought a towel and a change of clothes.

It had been a relief to sign the papers on the ranch. Andrew would never let her go now. He loved the ranch. She knew he loved her too, but she couldn't help feeling a little more secure in his affections due to the advantage of owning his home. Why did she always believe he wouldn't love her if she didn't have anything more to offer?

She knew why.

She had talked to Bertrand about the stranger she'd slept with all those years ago. He'd taken care of things back then, and she hadn't asked any questions at the time, but she did last night. He'd confirmed that Dave Park was the man who had attacked her mother at the hospital.

Nicole trembled now to think of the encounter at the airport bar as being a setup. Bertrand had said that the man's real name was unknown, but he was an enemy of the family. He hadn't explained further, even when she had insisted that he tell her everything he knew.

Bertrand did, however, mention her bruises after the encounter with the man. He was confident that she had fought back. He conceded however that she would have been easily overpowered.

It was rape. She hadn't wanted to sleep with that terrible man. Part of her felt relieved, but the rest of her quailed in horror.

She had become a statistic.

She had nightmares all night, but she tried not to dwell on it. She wanted to make it go away, to marry Andrew and sleep with him for the first time to prove she was fine, to prove she could do it without falling apart. But worry nagged at her, telling her she couldn't go through with it, making her feel like some post-traumatic figure in a movie.

Gripping the steering wheel, she drove up the switchbacks. At the turn-off to the ranch, she followed the road to the gate and beyond. She found Andrew working on the tractor in the barn. She could see him through the open doors and honked the horn. He dropped his tools, ran past her into the ranch house, and returned wearing a T-shirt and swimming trunks with flip-flops and a ball cap.

He looked good and the sight of his blond hair curling out the bottom of the cap and his broad shoulders and muscular chest gave her a thrill. She wanted him, needed him, and could actually wait for him. It was important not to push him to marry her before he was ready, but oh, how she wished she could.

He moved the picnic basket to the back seat and then hopped in next to her. That's when she noticed the scars on his arms. He had always worn long sleeves. A sick feeling unsettled her stomach.

He noticed her staring and rubbed his arms. "It's okay. They don't hurt anymore."

"Are those bite marks?" Shock numbed her. "Mother said you were fine."

"When? Did she come to the hospital?" He frowned.

"No, she stayed with me. I..." She shook her head. "She said you were upset that I'd caused you to be sent home from your mission."

He took her hand and exhaled a long breath. "You didn't get me sent home. I came home to propose to you. I love you."

She met his gaze. "Those are scars from Yar and Worf, aren't they?"

Guilt ripped her heart to shreds.

Mother had lied.

A range of emotions played across his face as his lips worked to find the word. "Yes."

"So, I did that. I hurt you." She was appalled.

He squeezed her hand. "I'm fine."

She shook her head and pulled her hand away. "How many stitches did it take to put you back together?" Anguish overwhelmed her as tears gushed from her eyes and she swiped them away.

"Oh, well, a few. No surgery though. It wasn't that big a deal. Bertrand saved me." Andrew cut short after that last bit.

She scoffed, panting as she struggled with her feelings of shame. "And if he hadn't, you'd be dead. I—"

Andrew took her by the shoulders. "It's nothing."

She met his intense gaze. Something gentle passed between them. She melted into his arms and held him close.

"I'm so sorry. I had a reason for doing it." She needed to explain, but it was still raw.

He stroked her hair. "I would like to know."

She closed her eyes. "I did something really stupid and...I was attacked while I was blacked out. I shouldn't have been drinking, but it wasn't consensual. I know that now."

Tension rocked him but eased after a moment. "Are you okay?" His voice was thick with watery emotion.

She lifted her head to look at him. "My family has enemies. It was a setup. Still, I played right into his hands."

"How badly did he hurt you?" Andrew was trembling.

Tears slid from her eyes. "Not as bad as I hurt you."

He pulled her close and held her tight. "So, you're okay? And we're okay?"

She reached around his middle to hold him. "I'm fine."

It was a lie that she hoped would become the truth through the power of the Atonement of Jesus Christ as he became her personal Savior. She'd set a date for baptism. The missionaries were planning everything for two weeks from last Saturday. She hoped Andrew would do the honors.

He pulled a tissue from the box by his feet and handed it to her. He then proceeded to use one for himself, blowing his nose loudly. She had to smile. With a bit more decorum, she cleaned herself up and shelved the discussion of her baptism for a later date.

Chapter Thirty-Nine

Nicole drove the SUV and her fiancée along the dirt road to the blacktop. She followed Andrew's instructions to another gravel road that led to Oowah Lake. With the increase in elevation came aspen trees, and many of them had names or initials carved like black scars in their white bark.

"Did you ever carve your name in one?" She needed to know if he'd ever loved anyone else.

He leaned forward in his seat and gazed out the windshield with his hand on the dash.

"Yep." He pointed ahead. "Slow down. I think it's that one."

She pulled over and looked at where he pointed. She sorted through the array of names to find an old carving that read, A + N inside a large heart.

"Oh." She blushed.

"I think I was fifteen when I carved that." He laughed. "I always hoped you'd show up here in Moab." He stepped from the SUV and stood by the tree with his hand on the lettering.

Camera in hand, she went out to lean against the tree, raising the camera for a selfie. They both smiled. With a glance at the screen to make sure it was a good one, she was dismayed to see evidence of emotional distress on her face.

"How come you never came?"

She flipped the off switch on the camera and slid her sunglasses onto her head. "I didn't want to encourage you in your cowboy pursuits." She looked at the camera in her hands.

"Why?" He still leaned against the tree.

"I didn't have any respect for," she swept her arms out and looked at the aspens and pines, "this." She strode away, faced him, and leaned against the SUV's front. "I wanted you to impress my parents, I guess."

He frowned. "You mean by making lots of money." He stomped past and took a seat in the SUV.

She sighed and went around to the other side, taking her place in the driver's seat. "I wanted them to respect you."

Andrew folded his arms across his chest and leaned against the headrest.

She put her hands on the steering wheel and stared at them. "I needed them to approve."

"Why? What did it matter?" He shook his head.

"Because Mother hated you."

"What?" His hands fell into his lap and he leaned forward, searching her expression. "But she was always nice to me..."

Nicole shook her head. "A sure way to know she didn't like you." She turned the key and put the SUV in gear. "Forget about it. It doesn't matter now." She drove ahead.

"I'll never be good enough."

"Neither will I, because Mother will never forgive me and Father..."

Her father's death had ended any possibility of her ever pleasing him with a high-powered career complete with the accolades of success she had intended to earn. She sneered at the irony of his scandalous death being the cause of her stunning failure to launch into her professional life.

"What did you ever do to disappoint him?" Andrew looked at her with creased brows.

She glanced his way, taking in his sober expression and the beloved lines of his face. She flashed an impish grin.

"I fell in love with a cowboy."

Some of the tension eased from his shoulders. "Oh, well, shucks." He affected an accent and stifled a smile.

Somehow, his love made everything better.

Chapter Forty

Nicole drove into the parking area for Oowah Lake and found a shady place to park. When she and Andrew stepped out of the SUV, the sight of the lake took her breath away. She hadn't expected anything as beautiful as this.

The lake nestled in a valley of tall pines. The aquamarine water lay clear and dazzling in the summer sun. People flocked the shores.

Andrew grabbed the picnic basket from the backseat. Nicole smiled. He must be hungry.

She shut the door, clicked the lock button on the key fob, and focused her attention on the small lake. Nicole moved from one vantage point to the next, all the while taking pictures until she was satisfied. Andrew followed her and set up the picnic blanket at the water's edge under the shade of the pines. The bank sloped, but he didn't seem to mind and pulled out the food and tableware. She watched him until he had finished and looked up at her.

"Are you ready?" He grinned.

"Yes." She laughed at him and came to sit on the blanket with the meal between them.

"Do you mind if I ask a blessing?" He folded his arms.

"Go right ahead."

After the prayer, she enjoyed the meal and his stories. She was glad to let him talk about the lake and the mountains and the miners and anything else he wanted to tell her. Honestly, she didn't feel much like conversing, so it was a relief.

To her surprise, the pasta, grilled chicken, potato salad, rolls, and pie disappeared until only empty dishes remained. Andrew packed them into the basket. He finished drinking a bottle of water before lying on the blanket, seemingly content to take a nap.

She couldn't resist the urge to lie next to him and snuggle into his side. Part of her still felt vulnerable. But when he put his arm around her, everything felt right again.

He fell asleep, and she watched his chest rise and fall with a regularity that matched the sound of his breathing. He didn't snore. She lifted her head to see his sleeping face, amazed by how childlike he looked despite the stubble growing on his jawline.

He amazed her. His trust amazed her. His nature amazed her.

She wondered what else about him would be amazing. That thought made her smile. She felt a little impish to be imagining him naked, especially when his body remained a complete mystery.

She laid her head down and imagined what it might feel like to make love to him. As pleasant as she hoped it would be, a bit of worry worked its way into the fantasy and managed to spoil it. What if she did something wrong? What if he wasn't happy with her? She stared at the lake until her eyes drifted shut.

Chapter Forty-One

Andrew awoke with a start to the sting of an insect. He reflexively swatted the red ant. In the process, he nearly crushed Nicole. Only then did he realize they'd fallen asleep together on the picnic blanket. Nothing had happened, but it still sent his heart racing. He should have been more careful with her.

"I'm sorry." He realized he'd frightened her. "An ant bit me. I didn't know I'd even fallen asleep. Man, I'm a boring date." He climbed to his feet and helped her up. Pulling off his shirt, he tossed it on the blanket and kicked off his flip-flops. "You ready for a swim?"

Her eyebrows raised above the rims of her sunglasses. He laughed as he ran and dove into the lake. The water stole the air from his lungs. He swam out before surfacing and gasped for breath while shaking the water from his hair.

"Oowah!"

Nicole stripped off her shorts and shirt, took off her glasses, and slipped out of her sandals. She tiptoed across the pebbles of the shore and stuck a toe in the water. Shaking her head and laughing, she backed up.

"No way!"

He swam to shore and splashed her, but she wouldn't come in. He had to get out or suffer hypothermia. The water, regardless of the summer sun's heat, hovered around freezing.

Shivering uncontrollably, he gingerly made his way from the lake to sit on a boulder in the sunlight. The rock helped to warm him as he hugged his arms to his body.

Laughing, she came over to sit on his lap, putting her arms around his neck despite how wet he was. The look in her eyes said she planned to kiss him, and he braced for it. Nothing could have prepared him for the heat of her body and the feel of her skin on his.

Aware of the people around them, and grateful for the chilling effect the water had had on his body, he indulged in the kiss only briefly. She was wonderful and a terrible temptation. He grinned and grasped her around the middle to stand her on her own two feet.

A family with a bunch of kids, towels, and water toys approached them on their way toward the parking lot. Andrew took the opportunity to ask the man to take a photo of him and Nicole with her camera. The man agreed and snapped what Andrew hoped turned out to be a good one.

Nicole spoke only after the family had gone past. "Thank you."

He put his arm around her shoulders and side hugged her. "Should we head back to the ranch?"

She blinked; her thoughts must have been on something else. "Sure, if you think it's safe." She put her hand on his midsection.

His chest rose and fell as his heartbeat pounded in his ears. "When will you marry me, Nicole?"

She leaned in and ran her hands up his back. "As soon as you like."

This time he embarrassed himself. She backed away enough to look down at the bulge in his swimsuit. Her expression was one of surprise and curiosity.

He fled to the picnic blanket. Sitting with his knees raised in front of him, he wrapped his arms around them. He forced himself to think of anything else but her until things calmed down.

He'd lost his cool. She had that effect on him. It always happened when he least expected it, though he might have expected it this time.

Perhaps they'd better have the wedding soon, very soon. But he didn't want to rush her. Besides, she probably wanted something fancy in Paris. He had no way of telling her how or when to do whatever she wanted; those decisions were up to the bride.

She stood in the sunshine with the lake at her back, hands limp at her sides, watching him.

She must think he didn't want her. He had no words to explain that it was all he could do to behave. How could he tell her he'd marry her today if she asked, and all that followed would be heaven?

Feelings of love didn't make his body lose control. He liked that. When he thought about her in proper terms, it was sexual, but not in an inappropriate way. It turned him on but didn't rev him up. He ran his hand through his hair as he tried to articulate how he might explain it, but he couldn't. He had never talked about such things with anyone.

With a sigh, he stood and walked over. "I'm sorry, Nicole. I didn't mean to do that."

She turned to look at the lake, taking his hand lightly in hers. "I don't know much about men. I'm not a pervert and I don't look at porn. The only man I've cared about is you, so I'm sorry if I'm ignorant. You don't have to rush into marrying me just because I want to sleep with you."

Her words surprised and frightened him. He took her by the arms. How could she always misunderstand what he wanted? Perhaps he didn't ever say things right, but he loved her and wanted to be with her.

"I don't want to put off the wedding. I want you to be my wife and I want to make love to you. Nicole, I love you. Just tell me when and where, and I'll be there." He looked into the lenses of her sunglasses wishing he could see her eyes.

"But I thought..." She glanced toward the blanket.

"I embarrassed myself." He shook his head. "I should have better self-control. I hope I didn't..." He shuffled his foot and let go of her arms. "I hope I didn't scare you or weird you out or anything." He looked at his toes.

"You're making me feel like some kind of seductress. I'm not trying to tempt you to do anything you don't want. I will wait until we're married. So, you don't have to be afraid of me." She started to reach for his hand but pulled back.

He took her hand. "I'm not afraid of you." He leaned in to give her a quick kiss on the lips. "It does help to know you're not going to let me go too far. That kind of splits the burden." He played with the engagement ring on her finger. "I hope you won't make me wait for three years."

She laughed and gave his shoulder a shove. "I doubt I can wait for long either, certainly not years." She gathered her clothes and dressed.

He shook the sand from his Moab Red Dirt T-shirt, turned it right side out, and worked his way into it. He found his flip-flops and cap and put them on as well. Afterward, he folded the picnic blanket and picked up the basket. Nicole snapped a picture of him, then she focused on the lake and took a few photos of the kayakers.

She met him at the SUV, drove to the ranch, and dropped him off.

"I'll be back tomorrow with the contractor." She waved goodbye.

Chapter Forty-Two

When Nicole arrived at the house in town, she went straight to the study to call her grandmother. As the phone rang, she drummed her nails on the desk. What could be taking the woman so long to pick up?

A servant answered.

"Sharon, is that you? Where's my grandmother?"

"Hello, Mademoiselle Nicole. Madame Augustine and Madame Moreau are on the jet, coming to you. Your mother is much improved."

"Oh, Sharon, thank you! That is wonderful news." She hung up the phone and ran to find Athena.

The two of them set to work in Nicole's room planning a wedding.

"How much does the bishop of Andrew's congregation charge to marry people?" Nicole had a yellow legal pad of paper and a red cedar number two pencil in hand.

"Nothing." Athena shook her head.

"How can that be?" Nicole was flabbergasted. "How does he make a living?"

"With a job. Nearly all positions in the church are callings and unpaid." Athena gathered up several bridal magazines from a shelf in the closet.

"So, Andrew teaches primary for free." No wonder church members were often poor.

"Yes. It's called service." Athena set the magazines on the table.

"Like missionary service?" Nicole was curious now.

Athena laughed and nodded. "Exactly, although missionaries receive a stipend while in the field, they pay in a lump sum every month. My parents had to help me with paying it because I didn't have enough saved before I went. They were super supportive."

"So, Andrew paid to go on a mission to South Korea?"

Of all the places he could have gone, why did he go there? Mother had always talked about it. Maybe he thought she would approve of his choice.

"Not exactly. Missionaries submit papers saying they are willing to serve a mission. Then they receive a letter from the First Presidency of the Church directing them to serve in a specific place. It's done by revelation. It's a calling." Athena nodded intensely. "I was called to serve in France."

Nicole sat on the bed's edge and frowned in thought. "So, Andrew didn't choose to go to South Korea, your church leaders sent him there?"

"God sent him there." Athena brought the stack of magazines over to the California king size bed and set them down.

"How did God know my parents would move to Korea?" It boggled the mind.

Athena laughed. "God is all-knowing. The rest of us rely on revelation. Now, come on, we'd better make some progress on these plans before the timer on the washing machine goes off."

Nicole giggled at the thought of a washing machine telling them what to do, but she buckled down and respected Athena's work schedule. Between the two of them, they hashed out a pretty good outline of events and the logistics required for each. Nicole made phone calls while Athena folded laundry.

After a few hours, the two of them lay laughing with a dozen bridal magazines between them on the enormous bed in Nicole's room. It felt good. Athena was genuinely happy on her behalf. Nicole sighed and rolled onto her back to watch the ceiling fan's ornate blades rotate.

"Oh, Athena, I'm so happy and yet I feel like such an idiot. I don't know the first thing about anything." She shook her head and sighed even as she smiled. "I've never felt like this before. I can't seem to keep my hands off of Andrew. All I can think about is the honeymoon and all the adorable babies we'll have. I know it sounds crazy, but I just love him. Every time I'm with him, I lose my mind."

"You're in love." Athena pulled a face and laughed. "And so is he. I've never seen him smile so much. You make each other happy, so let's get you two married." She pulled open a magazine. "We need to find just the right dress and order it quickly." She flipped through the magazine's pages. "It's going to cost you."

Nicole laughed this time. "I don't care what it costs, because I'm getting married!"

Hours later, they were still ironing out details, but the date had now been set for Saturday. They'd progressed to a notepad of paper along with a calendar and a phone book, for all the good it did to try to plan a wedding in Moab. Not much could be found. But there were plenty of restaurants. For the right price, they managed to reserve enough hotel rooms for any guests Andrew wanted to invite from out of town.

Nicole's list was short. Mother and Grand-mere would stay here. It was a miracle they were already on their way. They would be able to attend the most important day of her life.

Nicole couldn't help but over-prepare. She ordered dresses for Athena whom she had asked to be her maid of honor along with Andrew's three sisters whom she had called and asked to be bridesmaids. Andrew's mother and dad had been so excited. They had asked what they could do, but Nicole had permitted them to do nothing. She booked them in the nicest rooms she'd found in town.

She also swore everyone to secrecy until she could surprise Andrew with the good news in the morning.

"By the way, Athena, please don't tell Andrew about the baptism until after the honeymoon. I just don't want him to think I'm doing it for him. Also, I need to be sure he wants me for me." She wanted unconditional love. It was important.

Athena frowned and sat up on the bed. "I won't tell him, but I hope I don't have to keep the secret long. I'm not good at that sort of thing."

Nicole chuckled. "The wedding is in less than a week and the honeymoon is three days at the Grand Canyon, so it won't be long at all. It makes me dizzy." It was all spinning around in her head when there was a knock at the bedroom door. "Enter."

Bertrand brought in the dinner tray. He had a bit of a sour look on his face to have to do it himself when it was supposed to be Athena's job, but Nicole only giggled. The affronted expression on his face shifted to a smile.

"Congratulations, Mademoiselle. It's good to see you so happy again."

"When have I ever been this happy, Bertrand?"

"Oh, every time you came home from a date with him. You were giddy then and you are giddy now, though perhaps a bit more so." He left the tray on the table in her room.

"He's right. I am giddy. I feel like I'm sixteen and I just had my first kiss. I need to calm down and get a handle on all of this." She smiled and shook her head. "Except, all I want is to see him and that's not going to happen until tomorrow when I give him the news. So, back to work on these plans." She dove in.

Athena followed suit, but not until she had buttered them each a roll.

Chapter Forty-Three

Nicole awoke in the night to Bertrand's whisper. The room remained dark, but she knew what his presence meant. Something had gone awry in the house. She slid out from under the sheets and crawled on the floor toward the panic room's secret door. Bertrand already had it open and ushered her in as he quickly shut it behind them.

With the door closed, he flipped on the security monitors and paged the police.

"Where are the house staff?" Nicole wore silk pajamas.

"There was no time." Bertrand fiddled with the keyboard, adjusting the camera angles.

On the monitors, they watched what looked like a ninja. He made silent entry through a window that should have triggered an alarm. The intruder searched the house. The one clue the man revealed was the inordinate amount of time he spent looking through Nicole's jewelry box. Strangely, he didn't take anything.

The intruder didn't find the panic room. However, he seemed to understand he'd been outsmarted. Just before the police arrived at the neighborhood's gates, he escaped into the night.

The police said it looked as if no one had been there. If not for the surveillance recordings, they wouldn't have believed it. The intruder hadn't even awakened the staff from their beds.

When Nicole's heart rate returned to normal, she entered the kitchen and took a half-pint of ice-cream from the refrigerator. Bertrand joined her and prepared a cup of instant coffee for himself.

"How did you know the intruder was coming?" Nicole spoke around a mouth full of pralines and cream.

"I set up smart sensors. I tried infrared first, but I wasn't able to sleep. There are too many wild animals wandering around.

"Anyway, smart sensors distinguish humans from other creatures. So, I set them up throughout the neighborhood. Anyone who entered this property triggered an alert." Bertrand sipped the coffee and joined her at the kitchen table.

"How did you know to expect unwanted guests?" Her suspicions had been raised at the first sign of the intruder and his ninja-like ways. It wasn't a robbery.

"Madame Augustine's house was broken into a week ago in the same manner. She slept through the entire thing but noticed in the morning that a few objects in her room were slightly askew. She reviewed the surveillance recordings and found the disturbing truth.

"The man didn't find what he was looking for, but he searched her for it. She came to suspect your mother's crucifix. Upon investigation, the care facility had been breached first, though not Marina's room."

The revelation hit Nicole like a thunderbolt. "It can't be." She pulled the crucifix from beneath her silk nightshirt. "Mother has worn this my whole life."

She removed the cross from her neck. Pinching and pulling, it slid apart to reveal a tiny compartment. Inside, she found a micro SD card.

"Could this be from a phone?" The gravity of the discovery oppressed her.

Bertrand's expression closed. "I suggest you call Madame Augustine."

"She and Mother are already headed here on the jet. I tried to reach them earlier, but they didn't answer." She paced the kitchen.

"I'll do it. Madame Augustine gave me an emergency number." He pulled a smartphone from his suit pocket and dialed. It rang, but no one answered. "Excuse me, Mademoiselle, in the event I cannot contact your mother, I have another call to make." He headed toward the study.

"What?" She left the ice cream on the table and hurried after him.

"Hello, this is Francois Bertrand, codeword Medusa Breach, repeat Medusa Breach." His expression darkened and he faced away from her.

"You're the spy?" Nicole couldn't believe it.

"Not just me, Mademoiselle. Your mother and I work together for French Intelligence." He held his hand over the receiver on the cellphone, listened briefly to someone's instructions, and then broke the connection.

All the blood drained from her face and neck. "Why?" Her hands went numb.

"My brother, Benjamin, was kidnapped from the streets of Paris. He and his fiancé had gone out to dinner to celebrate his graduation from university. He was a nuclear engineer, and North Korea needed his talents." Bertrand's anger showed in the throbbing of veins in his forehead.

Nicole shook her head. "I—I'm sorry." She didn't understand. "How does this involve my mother?"

"Marina was his fiancé and witnessed the abduction."

Air, Nicole needed to breathe but couldn't. "And my father?"

"He was Marina's first assignment as an agent. She didn't mean for you to ever find out."

"So, she didn't love my father...or me?" Shock numbed Nicole's senses.

Bertrand smiled and shook his head. "Of course, your mother loves you. She loved your father, too. How could you doubt it?"

Nicole gasped for air and a flood of tears washed her face. "She got him killed." Glaring at Bertrand, she knew he'd been involved. "What happened?"

"I can't go into it, but you're wrong. We were doing our job and

Marc, well, he thought we were having an affair. You need to know, however, that your parents were faithful to one another.

"Anyway, Marc let the business arbitration fall apart. Furthermore, he said some things to the wrong people. He is the one who caused himself to be killed. He almost cost your mother her life as well."

"Why would anyone hurt them?" Nicole walked over to sit in the chair behind the desk.

"An old adversary caught up with Marina because of Marc's indiscretion. He is one of the men who abducted my brother long ago." Bertrand's expression darkened. "Your parents were sitting down to dinner, reconciling. Their wine was poisoned. The effects were rapid, but your mother texted me, and I came up from my apartment to the penthouse immediately. I brought a reagent that helped to neutralize the toxin."

Nicole shook her head. "Then why did my father die?"

Bertrand had gone pale. "I had to choose which one of them to help first. You have to understand there was little chance of saving either one of them."

"And you chose her. I would have chosen differently." Fury caused Nicole's fists to tremble.

"I don't think you would have. Your father's love has been assured all your life. But you don't seem to understand how much your mother has sacrificed for you. You need her more." He met Nicole's gaze.

She shook her head and walked to the room's far side. "So, this," she pulled the micro SD card out of the crucifix, "is nothing? If so, then why does the intruder want it?"

Bertrand sighed. "Mademoiselle, the information on that card is not part of what we do. What is on it is not for me. I think the man who came here tonight wants the crucifix because it is important to my brother. It was our great-grandmother's and Benjamin gave it to your mother. If the enemy has it, then he will assume that Marina has been captured. Such leverage would be highly effective to motivate him."

"So, she never carried information in this compartment?"

"Well, yes, but...I've checked that card already." He shied away.

She looked at it. "What's on it then?"

He took a deep breath and blew it out. "I shouldn't have looked at it. I wish I hadn't. Excuse me." He walked from the study to his quarters.

Chapter Forty-Four

Nicole put the SD card in her phone and wept to see old photographs of her mother with Bertrand's brother, Benjamin. The love in her eyes for the nerdy man with dark-rimmed glasses was something she'd never seen before. She looked naïve and head over heels. It contrasted with her mother's standoffish nature in later years.

Then, the thing Bertrand must have regretted seeing appeared. A sonogram. Tiny hands and a bean-shaped infant in black and white silhouette, a boy. The next photo revealed the outcome of that story. Mother, dressed in black, stood at a hillside cemetery. She was all alone except for the impossibly small casket and Grand-mere.

So, that was it, mystery solved. Nothing about Nicole's life was what she had believed. She didn't sleep for the rest of the night.

First thing in the morning, Nicole waved good-bye to Bertrand as he drove away in the SUV. He was meeting Grand-mere and Mother at the airport. Nicole departed the house soon after in the car, even though he'd told her not to.

She headed up the mountain to meet the contractor. She should have stayed to greet her family. However, the news from last night had made seeing Mother something she could not face at the moment.

Halfway up the mountain, the contractor phoned to say he'd be late. She sighed. That seemed normal. Who was ever on time these days except for her?

She pulled up in front of the ranch house and found Andrew inside making lunch. He greeted her with a spatula in his hand and a grin on his face. The normalcy of it reassured her that some things had not gone downhill, and she went on tiptoes to kiss him.

"I like your apron." She teased, holding back the good news about the wedding plans for Saturday until the right moment.

"At least it's blue." He returned to his frying pan of zucchini, yellow squash, and onions.

She made herself at home at the table and breathed in the appetizing aroma, hungry. She was glad there was no Spam. Outside two Jeeps pulled up to block in her car. Two black-clad figures jumped out.

"Run!"

Andrew didn't even shut off the stove. He followed her out the back door. They ran through the garden and into the junipers.

"Where can we go to escape?" She didn't slow down.

He surged ahead, racing toward the mesa's northern edge. He seemed to know where to go and helped her descend through a crack in the cliff's edge. It led to the bottom of the mesa. Once there, he pulled her behind a boulder.

"What?" She kept her voice at a whisper.

"I see them on the edge." He pressed her to the cliff wall and cocked his head to listen, frowning. "It's only a matter of time before they find the horse trail down here. We need to keep moving. If we stay in the shade, they may not spot us."

"You've taken horses down that?" She couldn't believe any sane horse would attempt it and distracted herself with those thoughts to keep panic at bay.

He laughed under his breath. "Every summer with my grandpa, since I was five."

She listened as he whispered stories about how Native Americans escaped a posse of lawmen this way. As they walked further away, he told her about how the mail route had come through here to serve the miners in the mountains. She held his hand as he led the way.

Hours passed.

She wondered why he didn't question her about the Asian men who were chasing her. Perhaps she should have told him everything she knew, but she didn't want to place him in further danger. Somehow, she had held onto her handbag and she pulled him up short.

"You need to eat. I have two granola bars in my purse."

He met her gaze and the argument on his lips died. "Thank you."

She handed him the granola bars. "How long will it take to reach safety?"

"On foot? Not until mid-morning tomorrow." The muscles in his jaw clenched.

"You'll have to conserve the food. Have half of one now and the other half in a few hours. Save the second granola bar for tomorrow, if you can." She handed both to him.

His expression grew pained. "What about you?"

"I'll chew gum if I'm hungry."

She remembered her smartphone and looked for it, but it wasn't there. She must have left it in the car. Her heart sank. Walking along the only way open ahead of them, she pressed forward.

Chapter Forty-Five

Andrew ate as he walked behind Nicole along the faded trail. It was hot now but it would be cold tonight. At least she had worn her hiking boots, long sleeve shirt, and sunglasses. That was a relief.

He had his ball cap, boots, jeans, and a long sleeve shirt as well as the blue apron. He knew how to keep warm and thrilled to think of cuddling with Nicole tonight. The food revived him enough to wonder what was happening.

"Who were those men, and why are you running away from them?"

"I'm not exactly sure." She avoided eye contact.

"Why were they speaking Korean?" He swallowed the dust in his throat, knowing when she wasn't telling him something.

Nicole shook her head. "Korean?" She pulled the crucifix from beneath her shirt and held it tight.

"So, you know nothing about why they're chasing us?" He couldn't believe that.

"I—I know something, but it's not related. At least, I don't think it is." The phrase *old adversary* came to mind. "Well, maybe it is, but it's my mother's business. Dangerous. I'm sorry to have involved you. It's good you knew a way off the mesa."

He caught Nicole by the hand. Her father must have died because of this business. Now, she might be killed. He marveled to realize her biggest concern was regret for involving him.

He embraced her. "I will keep you safe."

She hugged him, rested her head on his chest, and breathed deeply.

He chuckled. "What are you doing?"

She nuzzled her cheek on his shirt, "Listening to your heart," holding onto him a little longer.

"We'd better keep moving or we'll never make it to civilization."

She let go and gave him an impish grin. "Is that what you call it?"

He laughed. "Compared to this." He swept his arms wide to indicate the red rock formations and scrub brush underneath a wide blue sky. "Yes."

"Then keep walking."

They found water only once along the side of the mesa. But down in Hidden Valley a stream provided cold, clean water for them to drink their fill. This valley was frequented by locals. He hoped to find the right ones, people who would help.

As night fell, he cut pine branches to lie on and a couple to cover them with. He made sure to secret their sleeping place out of sight from the off-road vehicle trail that ran the length of the valley. They hadn't seen anyone. But with Nicole's life at risk, he didn't want to take a chance.

He'd already eaten the second half of the first granola bar. Concerned, he wondered if it would be enough to keep his blood sugar from dropping too low. He would need energy for the hike in the morning.

He and Nicole lay on the pine branches. He popped the snaps on his pearl snap shirt. She slid in next to his chest, laying on half of the shirt. He covered her with the other half. Drawing the blue apron and several pine branches over them, he wrapped his arms around her. Snuggled together and exhausted, they slept.

Chapter Forty-Six

Nicole dreamt of nothing until a weight pinned her in place. The sensation caused fear to gradually build in her mind. She tumbled into it and fell prey to terror. In the dream, a man held her down. She told him to stop and tried to push him away.

He laughed. That surprised her because people didn't laugh at her. He hurt her, and there was nothing she could do about it. The image blurred like there were two of them. Two men that looked exactly alike. Terror seized her.

In her sleep, she struggled against the assailants, but they didn't stop. With a start, she awoke, half crushed by a sleeping Andrew's dead weight. He had rolled onto her in the night. She could see because gray dawn had come.

Catching her breath, she realized it had only been a nightmare. But as details of the dream crept back into her mind, she realized it had been what happened in the hotel room with the stranger. She had never remembered it before, but the man's laugh echoed in her mind, ringing as truth.

It was real.

She eased away from Andrew and stood. It was cold, but she needed a moment alone. Had there been two of them that night? Wandering along the valley, she found a fallen log and sat to ponder things.

She needed to talk to Andrew about it. But what if he didn't understand? What if he looked at her differently after she admitted she'd been assaulted by two men?

The word rape was difficult to say. It made her question her resolve to become close to anyone—anyone except Andrew. He would never hurt her.

She tried not to fear the first time they would be together as husband and wife. But the simple act of his rolling closer to her during the night had caused her trauma. What if additional unpleasant memories resurfaced?

The sound of a vehicle roused her from her thoughts. As she looked up, she realized she'd already been spotted by a man in a Jeep. There was nowhere to go, and she had no strength left.

Andrew lay far enough away to be safe if only he didn't wake up. She walked toward the Jeep to keep the man as far from him as possible. Pulling the crucifix from around her neck, she lifted the chain over her head.

"Is this what you want?" Trembling, she extended it to Dave Park.

He jumped from the Jeep to snatch it from her hand. She shrank away from him. Drawing a handgun, a microexpression of cruelty darkened his smile. He had perfect teeth.

"Marina need's a kidney, and I can't let her have one, so I'm taking your spare."

He squeezed the trigger, and pain flashed through Nicole's middle. In shock, she fell to the ground. Dazed, she watched the Jeep turn around and drive along the rocky trail the way it had come. The sound of running water in the stream echoed in her mind until she blacked out.

Chapter Forty-Seven

Andrew awoke with a shiver to find Nicole absent. He didn't worry. She must have needed exactly what he needed, a handy bush to water. He found one and then washed his hands and face in the stream.

The morning was beautiful, and he sat on a rock to enjoy it. Birds sang as the light crept over the canyon's rim. Waiting for Nicole to return, he ate half a granola bar. The trembling of his hands lessened, but he still felt dizzy. He ate the rest of the granola bar to help bring up his blood sugar. He would need the energy to climb out of the valley to the nearest house.

The faint sound of a vehicle traveled the length of the canyon. He took cover behind a thicket of trees. Hiding far enough from the off-road vehicle trail to avoid being spotted, he hoped Nicole had done the same.

A gunshot resounded in the canyon, penetrating as if into his own heart. He ran toward the vehicle. The driver was already gunning it away along the trail.

Nicole lay on the ground, blood oozing from a hole in her midsection. He came to his knees at her side. Pulling the handkerchief from his back pocket, he pressed it to the wound.

She didn't make a sound or open her eyes.

Rolling up the kitchen apron, he tied it around her wound and tossed her over his shoulder. He prayed as he hiked the steep trail over the rim of the valley to the nearest house.

Disoriented, he lay Nicole on the porch swing at the first home he found. Gasping for breath, he rang the doorbell. A woman answered just before he collapsed.

IN AND OUT OF CONSCIOUSNESS, Andrew felt a firm grip on his wrist. Someone was checking his pulse. They found his medical alert pendant and loaded him into a second ambulance.

The police and ambulances had arrived within minutes. Nicole was well cared for and protected. The officer escorted the emergency vehicles to the hospital.

Andrew struggled against the oxygen mask and intravenous line as the paramedics unloaded him from the ambulance. He expected to find Nicole being loaded directly into a waiting life flight helicopter but none was on the pad. His heart sank as they raced her inside the emergency room.

He pulled off the mask. "Where's the helicopter?"

The paramedic gave a curt head shake as he and his partner pushed Andrew into the ER. "Corona Arch, some dude failed calculus. He probably won't make it."

It happened far too often. Arch swingers sometimes miscalculated the length of rope needed to safely make the swing. Andrew had never guessed there might be a cost to himself, but if Nicole died because of it...

"Don't worry, your friend is in good hands." The paramedic passed him off to the ER staff who soon had him in a private room.

The police officer knocked on the open door and came in to question him. Andrew related all the information he had. Unfortunately, he didn't know much.

"We'll find the jeepers. I've seen them around town." He handed Andrew a tablet. "Write your statement and sign it."

The glucose solution in the intravenous line revived his senses. "Her necklace is missing." He was able to recall details he hadn't considered before.

"Stolen?"

"Or lost. Is she conscious yet?"

Andrew hoped the wound wasn't as bad as it had seemed. Nicole's blood plastered his shirt to his shoulder. Queasy feelings churned in his stomach to see it there. So much blood.

A nurse had come in to take his vitals and overheard the question. "She's in surgery."

"Will you please keep me updated. She's my fiancé." Andrew's voice quavered as emotion threatened him with tears.

He couldn't imagine losing Nicole a second time. Blood drained from his face and neck. Lightheadedness overwhelmed him to think of the loneliness of a lifetime waiting to see her again. He squeezed his eyes shut and prayed for her to recover. He'd been praying all along, but now he prayed harder.

Either way, she'd be fine, because God had a plan. But he knew he wouldn't be all right. It would be too much to live without her again.

The officer cleared his throat. "May I have the tablet back? It looks like they're releasing you."

Andrew signed the statement with the stylus and handed over the tablet.

The officer sidestepped a nurse as she came in. She removed the intravenous line and discharged him from the hospital. Andrew walked into the waiting room to find Athena sitting with her head bowed in prayer. He sat opposite her.

"Is Nicole all right?" Athena wore a deeply troubled expression.

"I don't know. She's in surgery."

"Is there anything I can do?" Athena's face creased with lines of concern.

"Where's Bertrand?"

"On the way, as is Madame Augustine and Nicole's mother."

His prayers were answered. Nicole's mother would make her feel better.

"Thank you, Athena."

She shook her head. "I haven't done anything to help yet. What do you need?"

Andrew noticed her looking at the blood on his shirt. "Can you bring me a clean T-shirt?" His head swam from the lack of food and the stress of the past two days. "And something to eat?"

"Sure thing. I'll be back in a few minutes." She grabbed her purse and headed for the parking lot.

Chapter Forty-Eight

Nicole came out of the anesthesia to the sound of a voice. The anesthesiologist stayed until he seemed sure she wouldn't slip back under and then he walked away. She watched people bustle around the large area until someone came to take her to a private room.

She felt awful and exhausted but had no pain. The liquid dripping into her intravenous line must be taking care of that. The recovery room was nicely furnished. The nurse made her comfortable, but her only wish was to have Andrew here.

"The doctor will be in to see you soon." The nurse spoke as she left the room.

Immediately, the door opened again and in walked the doctor. "Hello, Nicole, I'm Doctor Griswold. How are you feeling?" He looked at the chart in his hand.

"Fine." She most certainly had never felt less fine than she did at the moment.

"That's good. I've invited your mother to be here." He waved for the nurse to allow Marina into the room.

"Mother." Nicole couldn't believe her eyes. "You look well."

Marina came to Nicole's side and took her hand, kissing her forehead. "I am well enough. Now, let's focus on your recovery."

"How is she, Doctor?" Her mother didn't waste any time.

"She came through the surgery well. We removed the bullet and repaired most of the damage. However, I'm afraid she lost a kidney, and we had to perform an emergency hysterectomy due to the damage to her uterus. The bullet ricocheted off her pelvis." He looked from Mother to meet Nicole's gaze.

All the air seemed to suck from the room. Shocked, the heat drained from Nicole's face and neck. A rushing sound started in her ears.

"Hysterectomy? You mean, I'll never have children?"

The doctor's expression sagged. "I'm sorry, Nicole."

"Leave me." She cast her arm at the man, forcefully willing him out the door.

He exited per her command. However, his backward glance of pity angered her. She gripped the blankets in her fists, wishing she had something to hurtle at his back.

Anger bordering on fury made her blind. It masked something deeper. Fear.

To her surprise, Mother talked in a soothing tone. The nurse brought ice chips and a sucker. Mother stayed until Nicole settled down enough to realize she'd lost everything.

"MA CHOUCHOUTE, WAKE up."

Nicole opened her eyes to find her grandmother sitting by her bedside. "Grand-mere?"

"I'm here." She reached for Nicole's hand.

"I thought you were still in the air." Confusion swirled in Nicole's head.

"I'm here now." Grand-mere leaned forward. "How are you?"

Nicole burst into tears.

Grand-mere hugged her tenderly.

"Did the doctor tell you?" In a way, Nicole hoped he had so she didn't have to put the horrible reality into words.

"Yes."

"I will never..." Nicole dissolved into tears.

Grand-mere's expression was one of sorrow. She reached for a tissue box and extended it to Nicole. The tissues helped with the mess, but not the heartache.

"I'm sorry. Your mother will kill that North Korean piece of trash."

"It won't change anything! It won't bring daddy back. It won't—" Emotion choked Nicole's voice.

"Say it, Nicolette. It won't bring back your babies." Grand-mere pulled a tissue from the box and wiped her aged eyes.

"Yes, and it won't bring back Andrew after I tell him, either." Exhaustion caused Nicole to close her eyes.

"You think he'll leave you over this?" Grand-mere's expression was severe.

Nicole found it difficult to keep her heavy eyelids from closing. She couldn't tell Andrew. What if he did not leave her? It felt worse to think of him staying out of pity.

She knew he wanted children. He deserved them. It wasn't fair to trap him in their engagement when she couldn't provide them as she had always planned.

"Have faith in him, Nicolette."

The words drifted into her mind as if from far away. She scoffed. "Faith? God has a sick sense of humor."

Grand-mere took ahold of her hand. "I've thought so too from time to time, but it's not true. God loves us. He just has to let us make our own decisions...and our own mistakes. Otherwise, there's no point to anything. All of this is your mother's fault, ma petite. She did this, so don't blame God."

"You actually believe in God, don't you?" Nicole was genuinely surprised.

"Yes." Grand-mere met Nicole's gaze. "Can you ever forgive your mother?"

Forgiveness was what Nicole had sought in vain for years. Looking into her grandmother's eyes, she took a moment to listen to her heart. The ice inside her chest had thawed, replaced by a soft light that radiated warmth.

Could she absolve her mother of guilt? No. But could she forgive her? The nuanced difference became clear. Forgiveness would be a gift to herself, but the pain was too fresh.

"I may well hate her forever." She couldn't deny how she felt, not even to please her grandmother. "Grand-mere, please don't interfere with my life this time. Let Andrew go, if he must."

Grand-mere went pale. "Then let's hope he is a better man than you fear. I'll send him in." She left the room.

Andrew being a good man was exactly what Nicole feared right now. She needed him to go because he could still have the family he'd always wanted. It would just have to be with someone else.

It was what she would have wanted him to do for her if the situation were reversed. She needed to make him leave. The realization numbed her.

Chapter Forty-Nine

A long-time passed as Andrew paced the floor in the waiting room. Thanks to Athena, he'd changed his shirt and eaten a hamburger. She sat on the edge of a seat and watched the people walking by.

Bertrand's head nodded once in a while as he struggled to stay awake. At last, the doctor came out and Madame Augustine came with him. What the hold up had been, they didn't explain. No one except Nicole's mother and grandmother had been allowed in.

"Nicole is my fiancée. I need to see her." Andrew still felt quite ill but he felt well enough to see her.

"She has asked to speak with you." The doctor gave him a sad kind of look.

Bertrand stood up, having thumbed in a text message on his phone. "Her mother is on her way back inside now."

The doctor nodded. "That's good. Please, excuse me."

Marina Moreau strode into the waiting room in an aquamarine dress and high heels. Adorned in gold, she swept past Andrew to stand beside Bertrand without a word. She looked much the same as he remembered.

Andrew chewed a fingernail as a nurse escorted him to Nicole's room. When he opened the door, her sleeping face was deathly pale. Approaching the side of her bed, he gingerly took her hand.

"She's cold." He addressed the words to the nurse in the doorway.

"I'll find another blanket." The woman went to the cupboard, pulled out a cotton blanket, and placed it over Nicole's middle and legs.

Nicole came awake with a start.

"Do you have any pain?" The nurse checked the monitoring equipment.

"Yes." Nicole did not meet Andrew's gaze.

"Press this for morphine whenever you need to." The woman put a button attached to a thick cord in Nicole's left palm.

"Thank you." Nicole's expression held her customary formality. The woman had been dismissed.

Andrew watched her hand, but Nicole never pressed the button. When he met her gaze, a shock of fear ran through him. She had a dangerous look in her eyes. He started to question her, but she spoke first.

"You said I'd be safe." She skewered him with an unrelenting glare.

The reprimand crushed him. Guilty, he crumpled like a paper sack. Facing partway away from her, he sat in a chair beside the bed.

"I know," he ducked his head, "and I'm sorry." He glanced at her, but she offered no forgiveness.

He put his face in his hands. "I should have taken you out a safer way. The trail through Hidden Valley is popular. I worried they might find us.

"If I wasn't hypoglycemic, then I could have taken you out a less risky way. That man would never have found us if we'd gone the long way." He gathered his courage to look at her again. "Did he take your mother's crucifix?"

"Yes." Nicole's countenance darkened. She shifted her glare toward the ceiling, laying back on the pillow. "You should go."

"What did the doctor say?" He'd asked earlier, but everyone had been tight-lipped.

"He said, I'm lucky to be alive." She shook her head and refused to look at him.

"Nicole, I never meant for anything bad to happen. I would have died for you." He meant it.

She met his gaze with a fiery stare. "Perhaps you believe that, but I don't." She pointed at a bag on the counter by the sink in her room. "Take it with you."

Numbed by her reaction, he looked at the plastic sack and then glanced at Nicole, but she didn't relent. Trembling, he walked over and pulled the drawstring to see her hiking boots. When he opened it further, he saw the engagement ring. Fixated, he stared at the gold circle.

"Take your ring and go to Grams'. You're not welcome on my mesa." Her hands clenched into fists.

Dazed, he just stood there. "Please, forgive me, Nicole."

"I can't."

"You have to." Tears slid down to his chin and dripped on his blue T-shirt.

"Take it or I'll throw it in the trash." Her voice quavered, but she clenched her jaw and stared even harder at the tiles in the ceiling.

"You're going to change your mind." He looked at her, pleading.

"Not this time."

He left the ring in the bag and Nicole in her bed. He avoided the waiting room on his way out of the hospital because he couldn't face Bertrand. It was impossible to talk to anyone. The worst part was, he couldn't blame her for hating him. He knew she wouldn't forgive him.

He had just enough money in his wallet for a bus ticket to L.A., though he'd have to hitch a ride to the bus station in Green River an hour away. He just couldn't face anyone in Moab. He would go home to the only place he had left. At least his parents would still love him enough to take him in.

Standing in his way was a cigarette puffing Marina Moreau.

"So, you're leaving her. I figured as much." She crushed out the cigarette in the sand-filled receptacle.

"She threw me out." He tried to keep walking.

Marina laughed bitterly. "She didn't tell you, did she?"

He whirled around in confrontation. "I almost got her killed. She has a right to be angry."

Marina stood aghast. "You're blaming yourself?"

"She's blaming me." He glared at the resplendent woman.

Marina scoffed. "She's falling on her sword so the Mormon boy can find somebody who can give him a dozen brats to pollute the world." She shook her head, trembling as the rage in her voice intensified.

Andrew was taken aback. "What?"

"She's letting you off the hook." Marina put a finger in his face. "You're a fool for letting her throw you out. You should have seen through it."

"What?" Andrew was so angry he couldn't see straight.

Marina fiddled with items in her purse until she found another cigarette. "I'm the one to blame for all of this. I wish he'd shot me instead. That's why I'm standing out here, so they'll end this."

Andrew frowned in confusion. "I don't understand. Are you talking about the Koreans who chased us off the mesa?"

Marina frowned. "There was more than one? Your statement to the police said it was only one man."

"I only saw one in Hidden Valley. But on the mesa, there were two vehicles and two drivers. What's going on?" Nothing made any sense.

Marina flicked a lighter, but it was out of fuel. Agitated, she finally met his gaze. "Nicole can't have children. The bullet took that from her."

His jaw dropped in shock before anger replaced the feeling. "You think I would leave her because she can't have kids? Well, I won't." He marched inside the hospital.

Chapter Fifty

Nicole repeatedly clicked the button for morphine. It didn't seem to help. She curled up in a ball despite the pain in her midsection.

She wept until she had no more tears. Mother had ruined her chance for happiness. All her life, she had been a lesser priority to the woman who should have loved her more than anyone else on earth. But neither she nor her father had been as important as a man and child long gone before her parents ever met.

The fact that Bertrand had been in on everything hurt deeply.

Even Grand-mere had kept things from her.

The door to her room opened and then swung closed again. She didn't look. It was probably the nurse.

Laughter filled the room, rocking her from her misery into a state of panic. Nicole turned in bed to see him, no, them. There were two Dave Parks. She hyperventilated as she fought to control her breathing.

The laughing man pulled a knife. "I'm here for the other kidney."

Nicole looked from the one to the other in terror until she realized there was a solid core of peace in the very center of her soul. It provided a place to hold onto. She let go of the fear. There was nothing she could do except choose to turn this situation over to God. A calm reassurance quieted her breathing.

"Answer me this first." Her voice came out steady. She met the Dave holding the knife's gaze.

He came up short. "I don't have much time."

"Did you poison my parents?"

He chuckled. "I didn't have to."

"Then why come after me? Why did you take the crucifix?"

"The supreme leader needed leverage against the physicist. Dr. Bertrand has tried to escape three times in as many months since his wife and children died of a fever."

Nicole frowned in confusion. "I thought Benjamin loved my mother. Why would he marry someone else?"

"It wasn't by choice. It's a way to keep prisoners in check. Leverage."

The second Dave said something in Korean. The first Dave nodded. He lunged at her with the knife.

Two shots resounded in the hospital room. Deafened, Nicole watched as both Daves fell to the floor. Pools of crimson formed beneath the bodies. She was covered in blood spatter.

Bertrand stood in the doorway, gripping a handgun. "I love you, Mademoiselle."

"No!" Mother raced into the room. Diving to the floor, she checked on Dave one and Dave two. They had bled out. "How could you? Now I'll never find him." She turned tortured eyes on Bertrand.

He dropped the pistol and walked away.

"Don't you care about me at all?" Nicole couldn't believe her mother's response.

"Of course, I care about you." Marina slipped in the blood on the floor as she stood up.

"Did you know Benjamin had a family?" Fatigue threatened to pull Nicole into oblivion.

Marina stood up straighter. "That's what they do, Nicole. If he didn't care about me, then they wouldn't have come for the crucifix. Did these men say anything to you about it?"

Nicole's hands trembled as the pain in her middle became unbearable. "His wife and children died of a fever three months ago.

He's been trying to escape."

Marina dissolved into tears. "Thank you for telling me."

Nicole glared at her mother until she gave up. "I hope it was worth it to you."

Marina gasped. Her head snapped in Nicole's direction. "Non..."

"Nicole, are you all right?" Andrew stood in the doorway.

He hadn't left after all.

The pounding of feet in the hallway heralded the entrance of numerous police officers. They slammed Andrew against a wall and handcuffed him. She couldn't stay awake any longer. A wave of darkness swept her under.

Chapter Fifty-One

The police took Andrew away from Nicole's room in handcuffs. She'd passed out. Reassuringly, the machines said she was still with him. An officer questioned him at the station for hours. Unfortunately, he didn't know much. When he'd seen the two men enter Nicole's room, he'd tried to go in after them. Bertrand had stopped him and taken down the assailants.

After Andrew's hands tested free of gunshot residue, he was cleared of suspicion and free to go. He walked to the hospital. At the nurses' station, he asked about Nicole. She had been moved from the crime scene to a new room.

"She's under guard until the morning. It's almost dark. You should go home and rest. She's safe now." The nurse was the Primary President from his Ward.

"I can't. What if she asks for me? I need to be here." He swayed on his feet, dead tired and hungry.

"I'll find you a pillow and some blankets. Rest in the waiting room while I order a pizza for you." She took him by the arm and led him to an uncomfortable-looking row of seats that formed something like a couch.

He stared at it for a while.

The nurse returned and handed him the bedding. "The pizza is on the way."

"Thank you, Sister Kimble." He sat on the couch to wait for the morning or the pizza, whichever came first.

After the nurse left, Marina Moreau walked in from the vending machine room holding a cup of steaming liquid. "It's hot chocolate. I thought you could use it."

Andrew raised his exhausted eyebrows. "Oh, the hard stuff."

Marina made a wry expression. "Is that you people's idea of a joke?" She withheld the drink.

Andrew sighed and leaned his head against the wall. "Yep."

She glared.

An elderly pizza delivery man entered. "Did you order a pizza? I'm looking for Andrew Leavitt."

"Yes, thank you. What do I owe you?" Andrew reached into the back pocket of his jeans for his wallet.

"It's already paid for. Enjoy." The man took the pizza box from the warming case and laid it on the coffee table in front of Andrew.

"At least take a tip." Andrew handed him five bucks.

"Thank you, young man." The delivery driver hurried on his way.

"Care for a slice?"

Andrew didn't wait for Marina to dive in. He figured it would be a cold day in a hot place before that happened. He flipped open the box and grabbed a slice of Hawaiian style pizza. Sister Kimble must have remembered how much he liked it.

Nicole's mother set down the hot chocolate beside the box. To his surprise, she pulled up a chair opposite him.

"Fine. It's my favorite. So, I guess I will."

She grabbed a napkin and selected the piece of pizza with the most pineapple. They both ate until there was nothing left in the box except the plastic doodad that kept it from collapsing in the middle. Andrew drank the hot chocolate. He refilled the cup at a nearby water fountain. Sipping the water, he returned to his spot. Marina threw away the pizza box.

"Are you staying overnight too?" Andrew held the cup in his lap.

"No. There's no need now that you're here." Marina didn't sit.

Her acceptance of him stirred his emotions. He'd prayed for it for a long time. But he still felt hollow since he was angry with her for putting Nicole in danger.

The police had told him the men Bertrand had killed were foreign operatives. The men were here to exact revenge on Marina. It had something to do with espionage.

"Were those men spies?"

Marina seemed to be weighing her words. "Assassins."

"That man had a perfect chance to kill Nicole in Hidden Valley but he didn't do it. Why make her suffer?" Anguish and clarity of thought surged with the energy the pizza gave.

"The two men were once six, the Medusa. At least that's what I called them. They were a unit of look-alike North Korean agents. Of course, I didn't know that until I'd killed one and another took his place. That's why Bertrand and I could never catch them. They confused authorities by being in two places at once and giving each other alibis." Marina sat, crossing her legs.

"What does Nicole have to do with them?" Andrew knew Marina well enough to know when she was leading up to something unpleasant.

"Bertrand and I are French Intelligence agents. We've been hunting the Medusa since before Nicole was born. Things escalated when Nicole was drugged and assaulted by two of them almost three years ago.

"She's guessing at the truth, now that she's seen them together. I need you to help her through this. I thought it was for the best for her to believe she'd had a consensual encounter rather than...what happened." Marina looked away. "Bertrand disagreed."

Andrew tried to take to his feet, but his knees gave out. He couldn't catch his breath or stop the tears. "You let Nicole take the blame? You let her think it was her fault?" Andrew punched the pillow beside him.

"I thought you loved her."

"You are a child." Marina stood and started walking out.

"You dare mention children?" Andrew shook with rage.

Marina faced him with apparent reluctance. "You can still marry someone else. This doesn't affect you the way it does me."

"Is that what you think?" He couldn't believe it and stood. "You've tried to keep Nicole and me apart for years. Why did you stop me from leaving this morning? It was the perfect chance to be rid of me forever."

"I'm trying to make this right." She spoke with a mournful intensity.

He closed his eyes as relief caused tears to fall. "It's about time."

"What do you mean?"

He met her gaze. "I mean, repentance is real. Nicole needs you in her life. She needs you to be present like you've never been before."

Marina tilted her head with a tortured expression on her face. "How could she ever forgive all that I've done? It's too much for anyone."

"What you've caused to happen to her has happened to me too. She and I have suffered more than I can say. Now, we're grieving for the family we had hoped for. But you need to know something...I forgive you." He meant it, though it was a struggle to come to this point.

Marina shook her head. "I can't forgive myself."

"You have to." He embraced her.

To his surprise, she hugged him fiercely as she wept.

"I'm sorry." She let go of him and walked out of the hospital.

Andrew went straight to the nurse's station. "Sister Kimble, I need you to check on Nicole. Can you do that for me? If she's asleep, just let her rest, but I don't think she will be."

Nurse Kimble glanced at several computer monitors and then nodded. "Sure. It looks like she's awake."

"I don't suppose there's any chance I could see her?" He needed to know Nicole was all right.

Nurse Kimble raised both eyebrows and cocked her head. Finally, she sighed. "I think that will be okay. Though, you shouldn't stay long. She needs to sleep if she's going to heal."

He followed her along the earth tone hallway to a sequestered part of the hospital. A police officer sat in a chair beside the door to Nicole's room. He didn't stand as Nurse Kimble approached until he noticed Andrew behind her.

"No visitors. You know that." Officer Jordan crossed his arms across his chest.

"Agreed, but she needs to see him. Ask her yourself, please." Nurse Kimble spoke kindly. Her soft response obtained the desired result.

"Wait here." Officer Jordan knocked on the door and went into the dimly lit room. "Andrew Leavitt's here to see you, Ms. Moreau."

An emotional voice answered, "Thank you, Officer, send him in."

Chapter Fifty-Two

The low-level lighting allowed Nicole to discern Andrew's haggard and exhausted features. He was in bad shape. It was not his fault. Remorse gripped her heart because she'd made it worse for him. But she couldn't let him see her true feelings.

"I thought I told you to leave."

"Your mother told me we can't have children." He pulled a chair closer to the bed.

Stunned, she could do nothing but stare. It was as if she'd been stabbed in the heart by an ice sickle. "I'm the one who can't—you should go."

"This happened to us, Nicole. It doesn't just affect you. It affects me, too. It affects our families as well. Your mother is grief-stricken. She apologized and is trying to make it right."

"Well, she can't. You certainly can't. I don't even think God can." That last part thawed the ice sickle because it was the most untrue and allowed her to mourn for her children...their children.

"Do you believe in God?"

She wiped her face on the bedsheet, considering her answer. "Yes."

"Then trust me when I say, he can make this right."

She closed her eyes. "I'm ruined, Andrew."

"Then I'm ruined too."

"But you're not. You could marry someone else and have a family. You really could. I want you to." She wanted him to be happy even if it killed her to say it.

"Maybe I'll go marry Athena. Do you think she'll have me?"

Pain ripped through Nicole's heart. This was what she had feared would happen. Sobs wracked her body as she pictured Andrew and Athena holding their first baby. It hurt so much she wished the bullet had taken her life.

Suddenly, he was on the bed with her, holding her close. "I didn't mean it. I never thought you'd believe me." He kissed the hair over her ear. "I was angry because I thought you were pushing me away."

She wept for a while with his arms around her as he whispered reassurances in her ear until she fell asleep.

A KNOCK CAME AT THE door of Nicole's hospital room while she was in the bathroom. Nurse Kimble was helping her to freshen up. It was the first time she'd been out of bed for two days.

"I don't want visitors right now." Nicole trembled in fatigue from the effort it took to do this simple thing.

Nurse Kimble stood just outside the bathroom door. "I could tell him to go away again, but you know he'll be back."

Nicole stared at the hideous wound in her abdomen and then dressed in a clean hospital gown. "Fine. Help me back to bed and then tell him I'll see him."

Anger flushed her cheeks with heat because the man wouldn't take a hint. Maybe he actually was as stupid as her mother had always insisted. Except that these days, Mother had nothing but positive things to say about Andrew. The hypocrisy was revolting. Physical agony caused Nicole's eyes to water as she managed to reenter the inclined bed in a sitting position.

Nurse Kimble adjusted the pillows. "Do you need me to bring you anything?"

"No, thank you." Nothing would make this any easier.

Nurse Kimble left.

Andrew brought in a bouquet of orange roses with yellow tips. "Where would you like these?"

"Give them to Athena." Nicole couldn't help scowling.

Andrew chuckled. "Grumpy." He set the vase on the stand beside her bed and went to sit on the window seat.

He wore jeans and the scuffed-up boots he'd worn on the ranch this morning. His hair was even matted where his hatband had pressed it onto his head. He smelled like hay and grease. It made her want him, but she rejected the impulse.

"Just go away. I have nothing to say to you." She gingerly folded her arms across her chest, avoiding the slowly healing incision.

"Athena has no clue why you won't see her, but I told her not to worry." He leaned back on the window seat.

"If you don't want her, then find someone else." The man was frustrating.

"A blond, maybe?" He looked straight at her.

She imagined the beautiful blond babies he would have. "Perfect."

He scowled. "I'd sooner castrate myself."

She met his gaze because the anger in his voice had drawn her full attention. The hurt in his expression held it.

"I'm trying to give you—"

"What?" He stood up. "I'm miserable without you. I've dated every woman in this valley. I've even been out with Athena once. You know that. None of them are you, so stop pushing them at me. You're all I've ever wanted."

Her breathing rate increased until she was fairly panting. "I'm no good for you. Can't you see that?"

"No. I don't see that, Nicole. All I see is you." He ran his hands through his hair. "I see you when I close my eyes. I think I catch a glimpse of you everywhere. I dream about you because you're everything to me."

A change of tactics was in order since he just wouldn't accept the inevitable.

She reached toward him. "Have you eaten?"

He pulled a chair over to sit beside her bed, accepting her hand. "Yes."

"When did you and my mother become chummy? She's your biggest fan these days." Nicole veiled her gaze, trying not to enjoy the warmth of his hand.

"Oh, well, Sister Kimble ordered me a pizza after the police released me from questioning. Your mother and I ate it together. Hawaiian. I guess that's her favorite. Anyway, she told me some things."

"She hates pizza." Nicole rolled her eyes at his confused expression. "Anyway, she told me some things too, but not everything." Memories of Dave Park at the hotel years ago caused a tremor to run through her body.

Andrew held her hand tightly. "Marina admitted her and Bertrand's responsibility for all of this. I can see she's sorry for your suffering, but I don't get a sense that she would do much differently."

Nicole scoffed in bitterness. "My mother has never put me first. I don't think she ever wanted me to begin with. It was Father who wanted children, well, at least one. One was enough to make him happy. I guess that's why she did it."

"They love you, Nicole. I know he was proud of you." Andrew leaned forward.

"I tried hard to please him. And mother too. That's why I resisted you for as long as I did." She shook her head, pricked by regret. "I probably shouldn't tell you this but I brought a Christmas gift for you when I came to Seoul to see you on your mission. Mother returned it to me yesterday." She pulled the small, black velvet box from the bed's far side and opened it.

"You came to Korea to propose to me?" He chuckled and rubbed his face. "I'm an idiot. I would have said yes to marriage. That's a whole different thing than living together. I'm sorry I didn't guess that was why you'd come." He met her gaze.

"I bumped into the North Korean spy when I got out of the Rolls-Royce to chase you into Jamshil Station. In the confusion, I forgot the ring in the car. It threw me off." She released his hand and traced the scars on his arm with regret. "I've been remembering what happened at the hotel after I left you in Seoul. It's bad. Worse than I thought." She met his gaze. "There were two of them. The same two who died the day before yesterday...I think."

Andrew took her hand. "It may not have been the same two. Your mother told me they are part of a special unit of spies who all look alike. She's been killing them off one by one. I knew your mom was cold, but I didn't think she was this calculated."

"He laughed at me, Andrew. That's how I know it was the same man...at least one of them was." Cold horror held her in memory's sway.

Andrew pumped her hand several times. Agitated, he went to stand before the large window. Staring out at the parking lot, he clenched his fists.

She shook her head. "You're taking it all in stride." She hadn't been so calm about it when she first learned the truth.

"I don't want to be the one to hurt you further." He stared at the horizon.

"Just be honest. You've always been candid about your feelings. Can you love a woman with this much baggage? A woman who can't have...," she choked on the word, "children."

He didn't look at her. "I want you."

She fiddled with the box in her hand. "Are you sure, because—"

"Yes." He didn't turn around.

Surprised that he wasn't put off, she looked at the wedding band she'd bought for him long ago.

A memory chilled her, pushing thoughts of Andrew away. She could almost smell Dave's breath on her skin. She was sticky with his sweat. Not just him, another man too. She shuddered and wanted to spit the taste of them out of her mouth.

Why had they bothered to kiss her when their purpose was to torture her mother? Why hadn't she been able to stop them? She closed the black velvet box and gripped it until her knuckles whitened.

"Nicole?" Andrew faced her. "What can I do?" He came to her side.

She rested her head on the pillow and raised her hand to caress the fresh beard coming in on his jawline. With a sigh, she gathered her courage. He might not like what she had to say.

"Give me time. I'm going to need some counseling." That was an understatement.

"I'll wait as long as you need." He took her hand.

She pulled away, unable to accept being touched at the moment. "I need space."

He sat frozen in the chair. "What do you want me to do?"

"Hire someone to look after the ranch and then go back to L.A. with your parents. You could go to school for a semester." She closed her eyes.

"You want me to go back to UCLA?"

"That was your plan." It was hard to stay awake.

"You were going to marry me, don't you remember? I wish you had said something. It was a surprise when my family showed up in town excited for our big day." He sounded hurt.

It broke her heart. "You did say you would marry me as soon as I wanted. It was stupid to assume—"

"Yes, I'll marry you...during Christmas break. I'll go back to UCLA because you need some time to heal. But don't lie to me, Nicole. If you're going to disappear, then you need to know that I won't survive it." He held her gaze.

After a moment, she took a breath and accepted his hand. "I won't leave Moab." Her eyelids became heavy with fatigue. Somehow, she'd let him wear her down, but at least he was going back to school.

Chapter Fifty-Three

Once Andrew reached his parents' house in California, he rarely spent time at home. By some miracle, he was readmitted to UCLA. He enrolled and started classes.

Working part-time for his dad's landscaping business, he mowed lawns and tended trees. When autumn came, he raked leaves. On the weekends, he took trips to the coast to stare at the ocean. He lost weight because he studied all the time.

Nicole didn't answer his calls often, which made him worry. Her physical recovery was taking much longer than he'd anticipated, but she said the therapist was good. He hoped so. Maybe he should talk to someone as well. His mother was a good listener.

The only thing that made him happy was spending time in elementary school classrooms. Seeing the children and focusing on their education made him light up inside. He hadn't yet visited many classrooms, but today he gave his first lesson. He smiled on his way from the building to his mom's minivan.

That's when he stopped cold.

Feelings of inadequacy overwhelmed him because his life wasn't good enough to meet the Moreaus' impossible standards. With a deep breath, he took in the smell of fresh blacktop from the parking lot. Once inside the rundown vehicle, he noticed everything was broken and the upholstery sagged. Grinding his teeth, he stared at the school papers and fast-food wrappers on the passenger side floorboard.

He was common, ordinary, poor, and insignificant. He was a fool for not aspiring to more. An absolute idiot for being happy with this life.

He laughed away the bitter edge of his mood. Blowing out a breath, he turned the key, put the minivan in gear, and drove home. Despite everything, he felt joy regularly. That is, when he didn't compare himself to Nicole's wealth and education.

He wished she understood the simple things in life a little more, but he gave up on that line of thought. The two of them were from different worlds. Chewing a fingernail, he wondered if she was just letting him down easy.

ANDREW ANSWERED THE doorbell. He and his parents had just finished eating home-cooked meatloaf and mashed potatoes with green beans. Athena stood on the doorstep in jeans and a T-shirt.

"Hello." He managed to say past the surprise.

"Hi." Athena handed him an envelope of antiqued paper.

Andrew opened it and read the letter. It was an invitation written in Madame Augustine's handwriting, inviting him to attend an undisclosed event. Though the older woman didn't explain what it was, she urged him to bring his best suit and come immediately to Moab for the weekend.

He shook his head. "It's Thanksgiving tomorrow and my mom needs my help." More than that, though, he was angry at Nicole for not inviting him herself.

Athena cocked her head.

"Look," he said, "the only thing I've heard from Nicole in all these months was a few phone calls, half a dozen text messages, and a check she signed when she sold most of my cattle." When the letter had come, he'd gotten his hopes up that she'd written him, but she hadn't even sent a note unless you counted the word 'cows' in the memo space.

"She's not strong enough yet to go to the ranch very often. So, my cousin Craig has been taking care of things. She's been meeting with a therapist this whole time, Andrew, and she's made a lot of progress."

The pit of his stomach dropped. "I thought she was okay."

"She will be fine. It's just hard. She hasn't told you everything that's going on, but I think you'll be happy for her." Athena met his gaze.

"What aren't you saying?" There had to be something big.

"I can't betray a confidence, but she has a reason for not telling you about it." Athena's color rose and she avoided eye contact.

He had a feeling he knew what had happened. It explained why Nicole had quit talking to him. She had met someone else and was just trying to break it to him gently.

"I'm sure she does." He stepped inside and swung the door to shut it.

Athena's sneaker stopped it. "This isn't about you."

His brows came together and his lower lip protruded. "What's it about then?"

She looked him in the eyes. "It's about friendship."

Andrew closed his eyes, wavering for a moment. "I can't watch her marry someone else. I just can't do it."

Athena shook her head and smiled. "I wouldn't do that to you. It's something else, something you wouldn't want to miss for the world."

After a few deep breaths, peace descended on him. "Come inside."

"We don't have much time." Athena waited on the doorstep. "Ask your family if they want to come."

He hurried to the kitchen to tell his parents. They had a family prayer and decided to make the trip to Moab for Thanksgiving. Everyone packed as fast as they could.

A driver with a stretch limousine took them to the airport where the leer jet whisked them off. Andrew used the flight as an opportunity to grill Athena about the event they were to attend. But she had reservations about telling him. He couldn't convince her to say more.

During the approach to the Moab airport, he used the lavatory to change into his suit. His parents and younger siblings dressed in their Sunday best as well. Athena hurried and changed, too. He'd seen her wear that flower print dress to church before.

"Where are we going?" He could hardly stand it. Why wouldn't she just tell him?

Athena smiled. "You'll know it when you see it."

Two cars waited for them. They ran out with their luggage to meet them. He'd seen familiar territory from the air. It was strange to be in Moab under these circumstances.

Despite Athena's reassurances to the contrary, a vision of Nicole marrying someone else ran through his mind. Madame Augustine wouldn't be cruel. He frowned. Would she?

What if she expected him to be the idiot with his hand in the air saying, I object? Well, he wouldn't do it. If Nicole was happy then...he'd be miserable.

The driver maneuvered the car off the highway and through the streets until they approached a familiar building. It was the church.

"Why are we here?" he asked Athena.

"Everyone is waiting inside."

Apprehensive, he climbed from the vehicle.

"You may leave your things," Athena spoke over her shoulder as she hurried inside.

Andrew walked to the entrance as people trickled into the redbrick church building. He led his family to where the other people were heading, breathing in the humidity and chlorinated smell of warm water. Could he be here for a baptism? Athena walked ahead.

His body trembled as he came around the door frame to the multipurpose room. Nicole stood dressed in white and greeted Athena with a hug. He could hardly swallow past the lump in his throat. She smiled and laughed, chatting with people as they offered their congratulations.

Seeing Nicole in white filled his chest with sunlight. All his silly fears fell away. He hadn't dared to hope for this. She may have rejected him, but it was more important for her to have found the love of her Heavenly Father. She needed the Gospel of Jesus Christ. He had always wanted this for her.

"Why don't you come in, Andrew?" Madame Augustine's voice spoke softly beside him.

He embraced the stately old woman, unable to hold back his emotions.

Madame Augustine squeezed him around the middle and laughed.

"That will do, young man." She smiled. "It's good you came. She never said so, but I know she wants you here. You are the one who planted this seed in her heart so long ago."

Andrew swiped at his eyes, but the tears kept coming. He pulled a handkerchief from his pocket and cleaned himself up.

"Nicole did this on her own. Are you sure she wants to see me? She would have invited me herself if she wanted me here." He didn't want to barge in, because this was a sacred experience.

"Receiving forgiveness makes one more willing to forgive. Come in, it's starting." The older woman entered the large room, greeted Nicole, and sat beside her on the front row of cushioned folding chairs.

Andrew's family left him standing in the doorway as they found seats in the room. However, he was unable to propel himself forward. Nicole hadn't noticed him yet.

The meeting commenced with a hymn played on a keyboard. A pair of sister missionaries beamed bright smiles from the row behind Nicole. The prayer, short talk, and a brief video about the Holy Ghost took place. Then, Nicole was led through the door into the entrance to the baptismal font. Brother Westwood, Athena's dad, was standing in the water. He took Nicole's hand as she descended the steps.

Andrew slid closer to sit in the third row. She had such a reverent look on her face while the prayer was said. Brother Westwood immersed her in the water in one smooth motion. She came up smiling. The spirit of the Lord in the room was so strong it warmed him all the way through.

She moved to shake Brother Westwood's hand but stopped halfway as she met Andrew's gaze. Brother Westwood didn't notice her hesitation. He shook her hand enthusiastically. She faced him and smiled. He guided her toward the steps and let her enter the ladies' restroom to change.

Chapter Fifty-Four

Nicole felt full of light. She'd just been baptized. It was the most right and perfect thing she'd ever done. Seeing Andrew there had been like a dream. She wept with joy.

His expression had been one she'd rarely seen and dearly loved. He was happy for her, moved even. This was what he'd always wanted. How had he known to come? Grand-mere. She always meddled.

Nicole dried her hair with a towel, brushed it, and put it in a bun. She hurried to change her clothes into a beige dress with black trim. It was modest and she felt comfortable in it. She felt comfortable here. She put her diamond earrings in, checking the mirror only to come up short.

The diamonds were easily three times the size of the one in the engagement ring Andrew had given her. He hadn't taken it back when she'd told him to. But he hadn't asked about it or put it on her finger when he left for California either.

She looked at her left hand reflected in the mirror. She had the ring on with the diamond turned in so no one would know. She switched it to her right hand, looking at her palm.

If he still loved her, then she would be defenseless. Her feelings for him hadn't changed. She knew she was no good for him, but she still loved him.

If he had shown up any other day, then she could have hardened her heart and done what needed to be done. He needed to go back to his own life because he deserved the possibility of having children with someone else. But today the Holy Spirit had smoothed her rough edges. She knew she would have to tell him the truth.

If he still chose to marry her, then she would try to convince him he was making a mistake, but she couldn't push him away any longer. She finished her preparations and returned to the meeting to hear the end of a church video. Bishop Jolly gestured for her to sit in a chair he had moved to the front of the room. A circle of priesthood holders gathered around. She caught Andrew's eye and used one curved finger to beckon him to join the circle.

His expression sobered. Without taking his eyes off of her, he stood and walked over to the circle. All the men placed their left hands on the shoulder of the man next to them. They placed their right hands lightly on top of Bishop's two hands atop her head. The words of the confirmation prayer were personal. She felt the most exquisite joy at receiving the Lord's blessings. God lived, the truth of it warmed her heart.

She had taken upon herself the name of Christ and promised to exemplify his teachings. Cleansed of all her sins, tears came to her eyes. She attempted to swallow the lump in her throat. She knew how much she needed to be forgiven. The Savior had sacrificed so much for her.

The prayer ended and the men stepped back. She stood and shook the bishop and each of the other men's hands. She held Andrew's hand a little longer and accepted his congratulations as everyone took their seats for the rest of the program.

Athena stood and walked forward to stand behind the lectern set up for the meeting. She looked at Nicole and then at Andrew. Her cream-colored cheeks blushed peach.

"Please, forgive me. I prepared this talk in English, but I feel constrained by the Spirit to give it in French." She reached inside the pulpit and pulled out a framed print of Jesus Christ with his hand extended toward several small birds on a thin branch.

"There is a story in the New Testament about the Savior noticing the fall of a sparrow. Now, a sparrow holds no real monetary value. But it is God's creation. He is mindful of it, delights in it, and sorrows when it falls."

Athena swiped at the large tears that descended her cheeks.

"Nicole and I have been friends for only a few months. In that time, I've noticed she consistently underestimates her value in the sight of the Lord. She's not the only one. I'm guilty of it too, sometimes. I think everyone is."

Now, Nicole couldn't help crying. The words washed over her like a warm wave of light.

Athena continued. "If we only knew how much God loves us, then we would never question our worth." She smiled. "Nicole, you have just received the Holy Ghost. Having the Holy Spirit with us is one of the greatest gifts God has to bestow. When we are worthy of it, we may know the truth of all things."

Athena cleared her throat, glancing around at everyone present who didn't speak French.

"In closing, I testify to you, Nicole, that you are a daughter of God and he loves you. If you ever lose the Holy Ghost, and we all do from time to time, you can find him here." She pressed the palms of her hands together and bowed her head as if in prayer. "I say these things in the name of Jesus Christ, amen."

Athena walked forward with the picture and gave it to Nicole before she took a seat.

"Thank you." Nicole touched the Savior's face.

The pianist played a hymn and the group sang along. The meeting closed with a prayer. A lavish Thanksgiving feast was served by the caterers she'd hired. Two men opened the partition to the middle section of the multipurpose room where everything was set up.

Nicole noticed Andrew lingering nearby, so she hung back. She wanted to talk to him alone, but church members moved freely around the room. The sound of water draining in the font distracted her. He turned to go.

She didn't even think. She just ran after him. In the hallway, she caught his arm and made him stop.

"Andrew..."

He looked deep into her eyes. She could see his pain, though the joy of this day was still evident in the smile on his face.

"I'm happy for you Nicole. You are an amazing woman. Thank you for letting me stand in the circle." He choked up. "It means a lot."

She wished she could read his mind. "I'm glad you're here. I didn't want to tell you while we were dating, but Athena and the missionaries were already teaching me the Gospel." She looked at her feet. "I didn't do this for you." What must he think of her?

"I had no idea. But I never thought you would join the church for me. I never wanted that." He took her hand in his and glanced down as he seemed to notice the ring.

"I'm glad you came." She pulled away, though she regretted it immediately.

"I am too. Thank Madame Augustine for me."

"I will." She didn't know what to say, but as he turned to go, desperation gripped her chest.

He walked toward the doors to the parking lot. All she could do was watch. Her feet wouldn't move. Light and noise from the multipurpose room behind her dimmed until the only thing she saw was him leaving her life for the last time.

"I hope you have a good life." She spoke softly. "You deserve it."

He stopped with his hand on the door handle and slowly turned to look at her with such sadness in his eyes. The depth of his sorrow surprised her. His Adam's apple rose and fell, but he didn't say anything.

"I don't blame you for anything, Andrew." She let her hands fall to her sides. "Life goes on."

"Maybe for you, but not for me." He strode out the door.

Stunned, she puzzled over what his words meant. "Andrew Leavitt, what are you saying?" She ran after him. "Why should your life be any different? You can have a family!"

This side of the church was empty of people and cars because everyone had parked on the other side. Andrew swung around to face her. His voice lowered as if by the crush of his blond eyebrows.

"I will never marry anyone else, Nicole. You should know that by now. I've always loved you. I don't have it in me to stop."

Her bottom lip trembled. "But I'm no good for you. I can't give you what you want. I can't be like all the other Mormon girls. Even if I could have children, I would still be different from anyone in Moab."

He blinked. With a slight shake of the head, he pulled her into an embrace. She felt a tear fall on her cheek but it wasn't hers. She looked up to see him crying as he stroked her hair.

"I love you, Nicole Moreau, not anyone else." He let go of her waist and took her hands in his on his way to one knee.

"Will you marry me?"

He always took her by surprise.

The words, *resistance is futile*, came into her mind. It was as if her father were here right now. She could feel his approval. The veil of heaven was so thin, she could almost see him standing behind Andrew.

"Yes." It felt right.

"You will?" Andrew beamed a brilliant smile.

She came down on both of her knees and hugged him. As satisfying as that felt, she couldn't resist a kiss. Running her hands through the blond curls at the back of his neck, she pulled him closer to her until their lips met.

She loved him. He truly loved her. She broke the kiss and hugged him around the neck.

"I love you," she whispered in his ear.

He laughed and kissed her cheek, helping her to her feet even as he climbed to his own.

"I want to take you to the temple in a year to be sealed for time and all eternity as husband and wife. But that doesn't mean we have to wait to be married. Choose a date, Nicole. Please, make it soon."

She met his gaze. "Are you sure? Are you absolutely sure you want to marry me? What about children? I know you want them."

"I know you want them too. So, let's adopt. I did service in an orphanage in Seoul on my mission and learned something amazing about babies. They're all different." He smiled. "Each one is unique and when we find our children, we will know it. We'll hold them, look into their eyes, and recognize them somehow. I want to adopt as many kids as you like, but it's up to you. Whether it's one child or a dozen, I'll be a happy father, a happy husband, and the happiest man alive to be with you."

"Truly?" A house full of children was what she'd wanted since she'd fallen in love with him.

"Absolutely." He took her hand.

A smile turned up the corners of her mouth as she shook her head in happy disbelief.

He leaned in, gathered her around the middle, and lifted her.

"Trust me."

She nodded, wrapped her arms around his neck, and kissed him until she believed.

Chapter Fifty-Five

Paris at Christmas time was a sight to behold. Andrew took it in stride, but his family oohed and awed over every iconic landmark. Nicole had decided that the day after Christmas needed to be rebranded after the trauma with the Daves. So, she'd invited his whole family to France for the wedding and planned it on that day.

Andrew wasn't sure it was a good idea. The thought kind of shriveled him up to think about physical intimacy on the very day she'd been violated. Maybe he should have seen her therapist, too.

Most of the pictures from the day of tourism with his family captured him chewing his nails with a distracted look on his face. Grams' was in a wheelchair so she could see all the sights. She'd patted his hand from time to time. At lease, he knew she cared enough to notice his distress. Mom and Dad had been too busy with his younger siblings to express much empathy.

They were all staying at Madame Augustine's home. It was more comfortable than a hotel and she had insisted they be together for Christmas. He hadn't slept much when someone knocked on his door.

"Good morning, son. Would you like to come down to open your Christmas gifts?" His mother came into the room and sat on the side of the bed.

"Sure, but I feel like I just fell asleep." He yawned and sat up, pulling the pillow from the opposite side to prop himself.

She laughed. "I know what you mean. I'm still jet-lagged, too.

Anyway, there's a breakfast prepared in the dining room."

"Can I ask you something?" He didn't have any idea how to ask his questions.

"Sure."

"Do you think Nicole is making a mistake?"

"About marrying you?"

"No, well, not that, but marrying me tomorrow. You know the history, and you know Nicole."

"And I know you. You're overthinking it. Let her have her day." Mom giggled. "Your day. The wedding is tomorrow. I can't believe it. I'm so happy for you, son."

He noticed the laugh lines on her face. In his mind, she was the woman from the photographs of his childhood. That woman didn't have wrinkles. She'd grown older and even more dear to him.

"Thank you."

"For what?"

"Being my mom." He choked up. "Thank you for loving Nicole."

Mom smiled. "I've always loved that girl." Tears welled in her eyes.

He nodded. "Me too."

ANDREW DRESSED AND came down to breakfast. Madame Augustine didn't rest on decorum this morning. That meant things were a bit chaotic. Nicole came down a little late, but in time to watch everyone open gifts. He loved the sight of her as she walked into the elaborately decorated room.

She greeted those who noticed her and hugged Grand-mere.

"Good morning, Nicolette." Grand-mere took her place at the center of the festivities.

Nicole made her way across the room to sit beside him on the sofa. "I've missed you."

That put a smile on his face. "Aw shucks, ma'am. It's been a whole seven and a half hours."

His cheeks flushed with heat to remember the goodnight kiss she'd given him at the door of his bedroom. She still loved him. He was glad because he wanted her more than ever.

She laughed and took his hand. "I'm glad your family could be here for the wedding tomorrow."

The feel of her hand made life challenging. She was a huge distraction. Because of that, he wasn't paying much attention to the gift exchange.

"You are the gift I want," he whispered in her ear.

She turned away from watching the enthusiastic children and the ripping of paper to face him. "Can you wait one more day?"

That was like a bucket of cold water. "Of course. That's not what I meant."

His knee began to bounce with nervous energy. The accusation was embarrassing. Of course, he'd wait until they were married for intimacy, and likely longer.

He hadn't seen Nicole often since he'd returned to UCLA for the semester. He'd missed her so much. But it had been the right decision. He'd earned straight A's.

Her physical recovery after the gunshot wound had taken weeks instead of days and she still wasn't strong. If she were, then she would have toured the sights with him and his family. He'd wished she were there the whole time.

She pulled her phone from a pocket, glanced at a text, and then squeezed his hand. "You'll be happy to know you have a new calf."

He frowned. "What?"

"Craig Westwood texted that a cow had a calf." A distant look was in her eyes and her tone fell a bit flat.

"I knew when I bought that heifer something was off because the price was too good. Well, tell Craig to keep the calf in the house so it doesn't freeze. He's going to have to lock down the cow, strap on a feed bag, and bring the calf in to nurse a few times before he should trust her with it if he wants to keep mother and baby healthy. Winter is a hard time for them." Andrew avoided eye contact because Nicole's emotions were still tender concerning children. Even though it was only a calf, he wanted to spare her feelings if it died.

She thumbed in his response on her phone.

Without meeting his gaze, she embraced him and then pulled away. "I have a lot to prepare for tomorrow. I'll meet you there."

He caught her hand, drawing her in for a brief kiss. "Please, don't go yet. You haven't told me about how you were able to clear your father's name."

She relaxed somewhat. "It was mostly Grand-mere...and Mother. I stayed in Moab, remember. I had very little to do with it. Though, it made me happy to know he was exonerated."

The sting of the accusation hit hard. "If you wanted me to stay with you, then you should have told me."

She curled inward, clutching a handful of his button-up shirt. "It's fine. You needed to go back to school. But it was really hard without you. I must go." She hurried from the room.

He followed her through the house toward the stairs. "Wait. I'm sorry. I didn't mean to upset you."

She faced him. "I thought I was all right but I'm not. Mother hasn't come to see me since right after the shooting. She's promised to be at the wedding tomorrow. It will be good to have her there. She won't speak to me about daddy. All she does is spend money and travel."

He tried to move closer, but she retreated. "I'm sorry to hear that because I thought she was opening up. Do you have any news about Bertrand?"

"Acquitted of all charges. I don't know where he is or if he'll be there tomorrow." She wouldn't look at him.

Andrew blew out a breath through pursed lips. "I hope he's coming."

She met his gaze. "Mother hasn't given up on her true love. She doesn't seem to care what happens to me. I lost so much because of her."

He hurt on Nicole's behalf. "You will never lose me, and I'll never give up on us. So, that takes the burden off of you trying to hold onto me. You are all I want," he smiled, "for Christmas or any other day."

"That isn't true for either one of us." She fled up the stairs.

SOMEHOW, ANDREW HAD managed to sleep. By 8:30 in the morning, everyone loaded into Grand-mere's classic car collection and rode to the wedding location. Nicole had kept her plans a secret.

He was dressed in a tailor-made tuxedo. The driver maneuvered them through the city streets until they approached a strangely familiar building. Andrew spotted the lettering on the side and recognized it, even though he didn't speak French. This was a Church of Jesus Christ of Latter-day Saints.

"Why are we here?" He glanced at the driver.

"The family is waiting inside."

Andrew stepped from the car and walked to the entrance as people trickled into the church building. A man in a suit with shiny shoes greeted him with a handshake in the foyer. Andrew walked to where the other people, including his family, were heading.

He spotted Athena walking ahead. She was wearing a yellow silk dress. She was the maid of honor. Eager to ask her why they weren't at some fancy wedding hall, he hurried after her.

His body trembled as he came around the door frame to the multipurpose room. Nicole stood dressed in an elegant, white wedding dress. She greeted Athena with a hug.

He could hardly swallow past the lump in his throat. Nicole smiled and laughed, chatting with people as they offered their congratulations. Well, at least that's what he imagined they were saying since many of them spoke French.

Seeing Nicole in white filled his chest with rays of sunlight.

"Why don't you come in, Andrew?" Madame Augustine spoke softly behind him.

He chuckled through sobs of joy and embraced the stately old woman.

Madame Augustine hugged him.

"That will do, young man." She smiled, giving him a wink. "It's good you were not late."

Andrew swiped at his eyes with a handkerchief but the tears kept coming.

"Nicole looks amazing."

"You don't look half bad either. Come in. We can't start without you." The older woman entered the large room, greeted Nicole, and took a seat on the front row of cushioned folding chairs.

Marina Moreau embraced her daughter. Nicole smiled in apparent relief. He stepped forward to come to her side, but her mother swept her from the room through a side door.

Chapter Fifty-Six

Nicole held her mother's hand as they made their way to the mother's lounge.

"Don't look surprised. I knew you'd go through with it. Here, let me help you with the veil." Marina unzipped a garment bag.

"Thank you, Mother." Emotion filled Nicole's heart with joy. "I'm grateful you came."

"There's no place on earth I'd rather be than with you right now." Marina smiled. "Good thing, you decided to be married in France, because I no longer have travel privileges outside the country."

Nicole embraced her mother. "I didn't know. I thought you were avoiding me."

Marina held on tight and kissed Nicole's cheek. "I love you, little one, so come see me when you can."

Nicole and her mother parted to look into one another's eyes. They both nodded, as a silent understanding passed between them. Then, they went to work touching up her makeup.

Family members and friends were already seated. Nicole held onto Mother's hand as the two of them walked down the aisle between the guests. Andrew stood beside Bishop Jolly from Moab at the front. Bishop had come to perform the ceremony.

Nicole took Andrew's hand at the front of the small gathering. Bishop spoke the most beautiful words Nicole had imagined possible for a wedding ceremony. She felt the Spirit of the Lord. Looking into

Andrew's eyes, she knew he felt it too.

She made her vows with God and her new husband. Then she accepted Andrew's vows in return. She had never experienced so much joy.

Friends and family rejoiced with them when the ceremony ended. Everyone ate a catered meal together and extended modest gifts to the happy couple. Life was good.

Nicole and Andrew danced. Well, mostly her, but he seemed to be trying. She laughed and rose on tiptoes to kiss him. He kissed her in return and smiled as he led her around the dance floor.

She had hired a photographer. Pictures of one and all were taken to commemorate the marriage. It wasn't as she had ever imagined it would be. Then again, it felt better, easier, and true to their new life.

She had decorated in yellow roses and fragrant white gardenias. The meaning of the flowers was to remember their love and cherish it forever. Even her mother approved.

Nicole held Andrew's hand as the wedding festivities drew to a close. They cut the cake. She threw the bouquet. Then, the two of them walked to the Rolls-Royce amidst cheering loved ones. The guests threw birdseed at the happy couple.

Dressed in a tuxedo, Bertrand opened the door for them. Nicole embraced him in a ferocious hug. Her makeup smudged his suit coat, and she tried to brush it off.

"I'm glad you're here." It meant more than she could say and her voice choked with emotion.

"Congratulations, Mademoiselle. Congratulations, Andrew."

Andrew shook his hand. "It's good to see you."

Bertrand nodded.

Nicole and Andrew waved goodbye to everyone. Once inside the car, Bertrand drove them out of town to a rented chateau in Provence.

NICOLE ALLOWED ANDREW to carry her over the chateau's threshold. They both laughed at the silly tradition. He set her down in the enormous house's entryway.

Medieval décor kept him chuckling as she led him up to the bedroom. Once inside she shut and bolted the great oak door. He flopped onto the enormous feather bed.

"I'm ready for a nap." He grinned as if he were teasing, though he did look tired.

She was exhausted from smiling and socializing but had no intention of resting. Could he sleep at a time like this? Surely not.

"In your tuxedo?" She hadn't moved away from the door.

"I guess so." He sounded half-asleep already.

"Well, I'm not sleeping in my wedding dress." She pumped an eyebrow suggestively.

He peeked through his lashes. "Oh? Well, who's going to help you out of it? There are a hundred tiny buttons up the back."

"There's only one on your pants." She had wanted to undo that button all day.

He chuckled. "It sounds risky to me."

She strode across the large room as best a woman could stride in a wedding dress. "I'm a bit impulsive."

He closed his eyes. "That's what I love about you."

She stopped at the bed's edge, feeling censure where perhaps none had been intended. However, she had no desire to talk about her insecurities. The last thing she wanted was for him to know how worried she was about making a misstep during their first time together in bed. The smile on her face was frozen.

"What makes you say that?" Her impulsive nature had gotten her into trouble on more than one occasion.

"You've been hurt, Nicole. I want to be sensitive to your feelings right now." His voice was soft.

The warmth of the moment stole away as if the men who had tried to destroy her life had the power to reach across time to rob her again. She didn't want to give them that power, but she couldn't figure out how to take it back. She didn't know how to undo the attack that now made her fearful when she should be the happiest.

"I don't want you to know the details." She had been working with a counselor but sometimes still had nightmares.

"Nothing needs to happen today. Especially not on this day." He stared at the ceiling.

"You would seriously not touch me?" Today had to be the day.

"It's too risky to do this today." He waved his arms on the bed, making an imprint in the down coverlet that looked a bit like a snow angel.

She shook her head and couldn't help but smile. "You're perfectly right. Tomorrow is probably too risky too."

He raised his head to meet her gaze. "What about the next day?"

She winked at him. "That would be much too impulsive."

Andrew stood. "So, there'll be no touching in this marriage?"

"That's right." She stood on tiptoes, coming a hair's breadth from his lips.

Breathless, he stood his ground. "What if you did the touching?"

"I can make that work." She put her arms around his neck and pulled him toward her for a deeply satisfying kiss.

After a long while, he broke the kiss. "All right, I'll risk it." He swept the hair away from her neck and leaned in to kiss her skin softly.

Closing her eyes, she enjoyed every caress of his lips. Resistance truly was futile. Tears of joy washed away her fears and freed her from doubt.

She met Andrew's lips with her own, kissing him until she wanted him, body and soul. Unsure of what to do next, she took it slowly. When he moved his lips down her neck again, she unfastened the buttons of his shirt to his pants. Breathless, she hesitated.

To her relief, he didn't notice her pause and continued to drive her fears away with his touch. When he worked her wedding dress down enough to kiss the top of her breast, that was all it took to banish her doubts forever. She needed to explore him as much as he did her.

One by one, the revelations that followed led to the most beautiful experience of her life. She need never have feared to make love to Andrew. They were perfect together.

If you enjoyed this book, then please write an honest review wherever you purchased it or on Goodreads. Your thoughts make a big difference to potential readers. Thank you!

Don't miss out!

Visit the website below and you can sign up to receive emails whenever S.V. Farnsworth publishes a new book. There's no charge and no obligation.

https://books2read.com/r/B-A-LKBI-FCBDB

BOOKS 2 READ

Connecting independent readers to independent writers.

Also by S.V. Farnsworth

Modutan Empire
Woman of the Stone
Monarch in the Flames

Standalone
A Rare Connection: Inspirational Romantic Suspense

Watch for more at https://svfarnsworthauthor.com.

About the Author

S.V. Farnsworth is a linguist librarian who has spent time in Asia. Issues with grit give her novels the traction to move you.

A Rare Connection is an international romantic suspense and a clean read. It is about a couple who met as children and grew up to live worlds apart. Can a well-meaning grandmother move heaven and earth to give them a second chance at love?

Woman of the Stone is book one in the Modutan Empire series. *Monarch in the Flames* is the sequel. They are epic fantasy adventures with an appeal to readers who connect with #MeToo concerns and admire strong female characters.

S.V. Farnsworth graduated with a B.S. from SUU in 2002. She teaches ESL at Crowder College in southwest Missouri.

She is 2020 secretary of the Ozarks Writers League. She served as 2018 and 2019 president of the Joplin Writers' Guild, coordinates their conferences, and edited the guild's 2019 anthology, *Seasons of the Four States*.

Subscribe to her newsletter for exclusive content and updates on her books at **svfarnsworthauthor.com**.

Read more at https://svfarnsworthauthor.com.